HIND POCKET BOOKS

Born to be Happy

Dr. Promod Batra (1936-2016) was born on 15 October 1936 in Sargodha a city in the Punjab Province located in modern day Pakistan. He was the eldest of five children and his father was an officer with the railways. As a child he was not exceptionally meritorious academically, but was blessed with the talent to learning on his own, think and find simple answers to questions on life. A habit which became his passion and then gave birth to his company – Think Inc.

Born to be Happy

PROMOD BATRA

HIND POCKET BOOKS
An imprint of Penguin Random House

HIND POCKET BOOKS

USA | Canada | UK | Ireland | Australia
New Zealand | India | South Africa | China | Singapore

Hind Pocket Books is part of the Penguin Random House group of companies whose addresses can be found at www.hindpocketbooks.com

Published by Hind Pocket Books Pvt. Ltd
4th Floor, Capital Tower 1, MG Road,
Gurugram 122 002, Haryana, India

Penguin Random House India

First published in Hind Pocket Books by Penguin Random House India 2019
This editon published in 2022

10 9 8 7 6 5 4 3 2

ISBN 9789353494162

Printed at Repro India Limited

www.penguin.co.in

FSC www.fsc.org MIX Paper from responsible sources FSC® C047271

This is a legitimate digitally printed version of the book and therefore might not have certain extra finishing on the cover.

Contents

Introduction

A few years ago I happened to come across a very charismatic man at a party. A high profile professional, he was enjoying the attention being showered on him by others. Playing the perfect gentleman, he was charming everyone with his pleasant manners and smiling demeanour. He was obviously a very successful man!

Watching him from a distance, I too was enamoured of him until he walked briskly to where I was standing to attend a call on his mobile. It did not take me long to find out that he was speaking to his daughter on the phone. His tone was impatient, almost rude. It was obvious that he did not like being disturbed while he was busy cultivating useful social contacts! I was amazed at the transformation. Behind the successful, happy facade, I got a glimpse of a man who was trying to please everyone except perhaps those who mattered the most in his life — his family.

When I reflected on the incident, my amazement gave way to a startling realization — we are so engrossed in fulfilling our materialistic dreams, desires, aspirations and trying to cope with our anxieties and "what-if" fears that we hardly have time to nurture and cherish our relationship with our loved ones. We often take our relationship with our better-half, children, in-laws and grandchildren for granted. Little do we realise that to be truly happy, we need to make our family happy!

I learnt a very important lesson from the man at the party. He made me realise a very basic fundamental of life — I needed to work on becoming a caring husband, a good father, a thoughtful father-in-law and a loving grandfather.

Each day is a learning experience for me as I make efforts in my own simple ways to nurture my relationships, with my family and friends.

Spending my most precious asset — my time — with my family has given me something I will cherish forever. I have learned to unwind myself from the worries of the day and enjoy the simple pleasures of life with my loved ones.

It is my ardent hope that some of my simple insights in this book will help you in making your relationships become nurturing bonds of love both at home and at the workplace, and if yours is a family business it will help you and your family to tide over the ups and downs of life — happily.

I wish you and your family a long and happy innings — may joy, tenderness and achievements always come your way.

Promod Batra

In dwelling, live close to the ground.

In thinking, keep to the simple.

In conflict, be fair and generous.

In governing, don't try to control.

In work, do what you enjoy.

In family life, be completely present.

Tao Te Ching

Love is the free
exercise of choice.
Two people love each
other when they are
capable of living without
each other but choose to
live with each other.

M. Scott Peck

ONE

Made for each other...

is it possible?

If you want happiness for a lifetime... learn to care for your better-half. Because caring for your husband or wife is what the two-way street called marriage is all about. The love and respect of your better half, with whom you may spend 40 to 50 winters, is far more important than a gold medal or a promotion or a step up the corporate ladder. As a husband, it has taken me several years to learn this simple fact of life.

One of my wife's problems, possibly inherited from her mother, is what to cook for dinner or which saree to wear. Earlier, whenever she would ask me for my opinion I used to tell her, "Why do you bother me? It is so simple that you can even flip a coin." She used to get upset. Now, I have become wiser. Whenever she asks me, "What should I cook for dinner?" or something similar which seems unimportant to me but is probably extremely important to her, I listen to her carefully before giving my opinion, keeping my fingers crossed. Over the years I have realised that she cares so much for me that she does not want me to eat potatoes for dinner if I had potatoes for lunch. I reciprocate this thoughtful gesture of hers by appreciating what she does for me.

In every little effort that I make to understand my wife better, I draw inspiration from Ganeshjee who thinks intelligently (big head), listens more (big ears), asks fewer questions (small mouth), concentrates more (small eyes), says 'thank you' (*ladoo*), is honest (lotus), uses nice words (perfume), has patience (raised palm) ... This has done a lot to make our relationship work. My wife is happy (66% of the time) and as she is happy, it makes me happy too!

1 There is no perfect better-half

Have you ever come across a perfect apple? Maybe you have come across one that looked perfect, but you couldn't tell what it was really like unless you cut it. It may be rotten inside. When you buy an apple with a spot or two wouldn't it be simple to cut that out with a knife? Please do not misunderstand me; I am simply saying that you can never get a perfect apple.

> **Marriage has its good side. It teaches you loyalty, forbearance, tolerance, self-restraint, and other valuable qualities you wouldn't need if you stayed single.**
>
> *Pease*

It is highly unlikely that a man will get a perfect wife or a woman will get a perfect husband. Use your mental knife to cut out your better-half s bad points and you will find him or her too good to be true. Fortunately, God has made our minds such that our mental floppies can be partially erased at will and only what we want to remember can remain in it. Try it out. This can lead to happiness in your married life.

Be a Pygmalion

The "Pygmalion effect" is most applicable between a

husband and a wife. Pygmalion was a character in Greek mythology who believed so strongly in the beauty of the statue he had carved that it came to life.

The first step towards a good relationship with your better-half is — have confidence in him or her. If *you* don't have confidence in your spouse, no one else will have confidence in your better-half. If you think your spouse is a pygmy, you can be sure that your better-half will become one over the years. Your opinion of your better-half influences his or her behaviour — especially in your presence. You can have a better-half who is twelve feet or twelve inches tall. The choice is yours.

Your better-half is unique

Very little is needed to make your better-half feel great. It costs almost nothing. You don't have to gift a designer wrist watch, or a diamond ring — just a smile, a wink, a kiss, anyone or all of them (not necessarily in that order) — that is it! Your partner will feel eleven feet tall. Try. And you don't even have to do it daily, maybe once a week, once a month — even once a year.

> **Nobody is happy all the time but that is no excuse for being miserable.**
> *Anonymous*

You must realise that to be happy, you must have a happy better-half. On the inside your spouse is like a little child who wants to be pampered; on the outside, he or she is the man or woman of the family. One thing is sure, you can't change your better-half. Therefore, accept your better-half as he or she is. If you *still* want to try changing a few things which you don't like, do it gently over a few years.

Always remember that your better-half is unique so treat him or her as such. Think of all the little things you can do for your better-half. Thoughtful gestures can make your partner feel loved and cared for.

> **You ought to believe something in life, believe that thing so fervently that you will stand up with it till the end of your days...**
>
> *Martin Luther King*

2

Making your better-half happy is an art

Many husbands feel that it is almost impossible to make one's wife happy. Perhaps it is possible to make her happy during the first three years of marriage or later during the retirement years. Of course, there is a very simple solution and one which is very easy to follow, though I have a feeling that God intentionally programmed our minds against it — and that is, in the words of Sir Homi Mody: *"There is always a perfect understanding between me and my wife. Whenever we disagree, she goes her own way and I go after her."* This reminds me of the story of Henry Ford, who in his seventies, after the death of his son Edsal, wanted the Ford Company to be taken over by his manager. His wife, Clara Ford threatened to leave him and go to her parents. It worked. He decided to hand over the company to his grandson Henry who was only 28 then. The rest is history.

When men and women are able to respect and accept their differences then love has a chance to blossom.
Gray

I do not know about you but I would not like to have a wife who is boring, who appreciates any saree I buy for her whether or not she likes it, and who does not pull me up at least three times a day. Do you know that in the USA there are restaurants that boldly advertise *"homely breakfasts"* which occasionally include burnt toast, spilled coffee and grouchy waitresses because research has shown that after a few days of travelling an executive starts missing his wife and these *"homely breakfasts"* remind him of his wife.

The idea of making your better-half happy is a very challenging one. To be with a person for 50 years, buddy, *you better learn to make him or her happy because it is only then that you will also be happy.* Everyday I have to make efforts to make my wife happy. I am sure it is the same with most people...

Let me share with you some of the research which I have carried out on the subject of how to make your better-half happy.

Do it now

Make common sense your best friend. For your wife, visiting your daughter's school teacher is more important than calling upon the Chief Engineer for a possible sale of six tractors. The Tiger vs. Mosquito lesson is relevant: you may not be able to concentrate on shooting a tiger unless you kill all the mosquitoes first. For example, if it is a question of depositing the school fees for your children, follow the concept *"Do important jobs now before they become urgent."* Send the school fees one month in advance and that too through demand drafts. I have seen many fights in the family because of delays.

Keep your "Do it now" pad handy to write down what your better-half would like you to do. A smile on the face of your spouse can be more valuable than an extra hour at your office.

Don't expect gratitude

I have never come across better advice than from my Guru, Andrew Carnegie. If you gave one of your relatives a million dollars, would you expect him to be grateful? Andrew Carnegie did just that. But if Andrew Carnegie had come back from the grave a little while later, he would have been shocked to find this relative cursing him as Old Andy had left 365 million dollars to public charities and had cut him off with "one measly million," as he put it.

> **Gift your wife a diamond necklace and she will say she always wanted an emerald one!**

Don't expect gratitude from your better-half, because it is natural for people to forget to be grateful. And if you ever get it, consider it a matrimonial medal. Whenever you do something for your better-half, do it for the inner joy of giving. Start being grateful for whatever your spouse does for you and it is possible that your better-half may get the hint.

Admit your mistakes gracefully

Admit your mistakes gracefully and you will not go wrong. Between you and me, tell me, what difference does it make if you say sorry to your better-half even if you think that your spouse is wrong to the extent of 70 per cent. Theoretically speaking, in life, between husband and wife it hardly matters who is right and who is wrong because eventually both get hurt. If your better-half reciprocates occasionally by saying sorry, will it not be music to your ears?

Mistakes are the best teachers, therefore, learn from every incident which makes your better-half unhappy. Find out what was the basic reason for his or her unhappiness at a given point of time. In all likelihood it could have been some silly reason.

Be in good humour

Assuming that you are going to live for 75 years — plus or minus 10 years — and further assuming that you are going to get married at the age of 25, you will be with your better-half for 50 years — plus or minus 10 years. Right?

So, why not be in good humour. There is a very thoughtful saying; *"I had the blues, because I had no shoes, until upon the street I met a man who had no feet."* Think of all we have to be grateful for, and thank God for all our boons and bounties. Think, thank and smile.

A smile is a curve which can set a lot of things straight.
Phyllis Diller

Smiling is infectious. In the beginning your better-half may wonder about your motive. But don't worry — let the smile come out of your head and heart. Start whistling — this helps! Think of all the pleasant friends you have — I have friends whose very thought makes me feel happy and younger. And yes, let it be engraved on the screen of your mind: *"A smile is an inexpensive way to make your better-half happy."*

3

Thank god for giving you a romantic better-half

If you want happiness for a lifetime... learn to love your better-half, every minute. I know of a husband who gives a flower to his wife as soon as he gets up. And the wife says, "*What are you doing? What will the children think? Why not offer these to Bhagwanjee...*"

Well, if you are a wife like this, think twice. Erase the mental tape which gives you such thoughts. Say a warm thank you, and offer a one minute silent prayer to God for giving you such a good husband. Learn to appreciate every thoughtful gesture from your husband. Think of such gestures as the bonuses of life.

> **Never forget that a woman is a romantic. She enjoys wine, flowers, and chocolate. Let her know that you, too, remember these things... by speaking of them occasionally.**
>
> *Woody Allen*

If your better-half becomes more and more romantic as the years go by due to the movies, books, friends, reflections — whatever — thank your stars! Remember, the romance of a house can continue as long as a husband performs towards his wife those little acts of courtesy that he gladly offered her in the happy days of courtship; and as long as a wife acknowledges these acts with grace.

Follow the Holi concept with your wife

Lord Krishna used to play Holi with the *gopis* and this sounds so romantic even today. A husband should do the same, but only with his wife. How? It is simple. Pay her compliments and appreciate what you may have so far taken for granted. For example, if your wife gets up at 6 a.m. to prepare breakfast for you and your children, say something like: *"I am so happy that I married you... I know many women who do not even get up by 9 o'clock."*

Remember to call her "*Deviji*" or "Darling" up to 3 p.m. and *"Begum"* or "Honey" after that... or any other variation that you can think of. Possibly, she will start calling you (and may even treat you as) *Devtajee* or *Sarkar*! However, even if you appreciate whatever she does, you should also be prepared for her not reciprocating as generously or as often as you would wish her to do. But it is always worth trying.

On the festival of Holi, when you sprinkle perfumed or coloured water on somebody, he or she may reciprocate with something similar but definitely not with used engine oil. My own experience tells me that you can follow the Holi concept with your wife at least six times a day; but don't overdo it. And also ignore her initial surprise!

4

Don’t take your relationship for granted

Do a self-audit every Saturday

Each one of us has a goal — to be happy in life. I sincerely believe that you should get happiness out of your work or you’ll never know what happiness is. When someone loves what he or she does for a living, it does not remain only work but becomes work-cum-play. If you love your work, it will make you happy. And if you are happy, you can make your better-half happy too.

If you’re a working woman start enjoying your own work, and in any case make sure your husband enjoys his work. Your interest in his work can make a big difference to him. So, start taking interest intelligently. It will go a long way in making your husband happy.

If you happen to be a housewife, learn to enjoy your household chores. When your spouse comes home from the office, for the sake of your own happiness, don’t throw tantrums. Grow up and learn to solve your own problems instead of telling him about the silly little difficulties of the day.

Make it a rule not to tell your husband anything unpleasant for the first ninety minutes after he arrives. The heavens won’t fall! Your husband can fight the world of bayonets, but not your *choon choon, bhaon bhaon.* He becomes a *bheegi billi* when you start shouting and getting upset. Your husband wants peace of mind when he comes home and, therefore, he tries very hard not to retaliate, and to accept insults and humiliations.

Don't take your relationship with your better-half for granted. Think of all the good times both of you have spent together. Never let your spouse feel that you have no time for him or her.

> **It is difficult for a man to listen to a woman when she is unhappy or disappointed because he feels like a failure.**
>
> *Gray*

Don't nag. Don't shout. Don't pester. Don't talk about household problems when your better-half is in a hurry. Use soft music, soft lighting, flowers. Let your better-half feel relaxed and wanted by listening patiently to whatever is happening in his or her life. It is a simple way of making your spouse feel great!

So, whether you are a husband or a wife, doing a self-audit is perhaps the most important step towards improving your relationship with your spouse. Do a self-audit every Saturday at 11 a.m. and reflect on how you behaved with your better-half through the week. Make a mental note of your blind spots and do everything you can to overcome them during the week.

On a Sunday, do only what you both have been wanting to do... together. Learn to enjoy the simple pleasures of life. On Saturday you had reviewed the week; now discuss it with your partner and clear the misunderstandings. This will go a long way in making you a happier, more satisfied and confident couple.

5

Draw your own *Lakshmana rekhas*

Greed can never be met

Sita: "Oh! Look! What a lovely deer!"

Lakshmana: "That deer is too wonderful to be real. Look, how it shines! It could only be a Rakshasa!"

Sita (ignoring Lakshmana's words) : "Is it not beautiful, Rama! Will you get it for me? "

Rama : "Certainly, my dear."

Well, possibly this was the dialogue that started an epic series of events! When I think about it in today's context, I can't help but think that Sita must have nagged Rama long enough for him to agree eventually to go after the deer, knowing fully well that it was a *mayajaal* (hypnotic trap).

When greed sets in, even *Lakshmana rekhas* don't work. We find ways to justify breaking them. Only you can decide how you want to live — to meet need or greed. While need can be met, greed can never be satiated!

There was once a very good, honest man, minding his own business and looking after his family very well. His company sent him on tour and he had very important papers in his briefcase. When he got tired while travelling, he decided to take a break on a river bridge. Suddenly his briefcase fell into the river.

Though a grown-up man, he started crying because the briefcase, which was made of rexine, contained very valuable papers. He thought of committing suicide by jumping into the river. Suddenly, the River God appeared and heard his story. He took pity on the man, dived into the river, and brought out a leather briefcase, but the man refused to take it as it was not his briefcase. The God dived in again and brought out a VIP briefcase. Again the good man refused to take it as it was not his briefcase. The God dived in again. This time he brought out the rexine briefcase. The man was very happy and thanked the River God from the bottom of his heart. The God was pleased with the man's honesty and gave him all the three briefcases.

> **I suggest that it is your judgments which keep you from joy, and your expectations which make you unhappy.**
>
> *Neale Donald Walsch*

Happily, the man went home and told his wife what had happened. The wife was upset at his honesty and wanted to meet the God who was so liberal! The husband had no choice but to take his wife to the bridge. Both of them sat on the bridge, and suddenly the wife fell into the river. Again the man started crying. The River God appeared and listened to his story. The God dived down, brought out Hema Malini, and asked the man if she was his wife. The honest man said — yes!

The all-knowing God was not surprised, but still he asked the question, "Son, you are an honest man. Why are you not telling the truth?"

The man replied, "Dear God, if I had said no, you would have gone down and would have brought up Rekha and if I had again said no, you would have gone done and brought up my wife and I would have said yes — and then you would have given me all three ladies. You can imagine my plight. Therefore, I decided to use a bit of common sense and be dishonest."

> **Love, truth, and the courage to do what is right should be our own guideposts on this lifelong journey.**
>
> *Coretta Scott King*

This is a story with a strong moral for wives. As a wife, you are more intelligent than your husband — in certain ways. If you want to make your married life a happy one, always tell the truth; and always help your husband to remain truthful even if it means living with less luxury. Your role is to help your husband to find relaxation, not an escape. You have to help him to slow down, and to enjoy what both of you already have. Encourage your husband to share his concerns with you.

Both the husband and wife have a common goal — to be happy in life together. This does not mean that both of them have to use the same path, or the same speed to reach their goals. Both can run alongside each other, or go the way each of them wants to, at their own individual paces — happily.

6

Tackle your partner's problems... together

Do you have a spouse who is a nervous wreck or is jealous or stressful? Well, do something about it. You are 60 per cent to blame for it!

The following Sufi story may help you to deal better with your partner's problems.

Once there was a rug merchant. He noticed a large bump in his drawing room carpet. He was puzzled, and in a reflex action he jumped on it and the bump disappeared. He was happy. But soon the bump appeared at a different place. He jumped on it again and again. The bump kept reappearing. Again in a reflex action, he started rolling up the carpet and an angry snake dashed out.

> **If you carefully consider the problems people face in marriage, you will find that in almost every case they arise out of conflicting role expectations and problem-solving strategies.**
>
> *Covey*

You may be puzzled by your better-half's attitude and behaviour. You may be using the usual solutions — nagging, getting angry, throwing tantrums, shouting, bickering. Your better-half's problems are like "the snake" in the story. They keep recurring.

You start blaming others — including your in-laws for raising your better-half badly. The fact is, there is no outsider! It is you and your partner who have created problems and only both of you can solve them together.

Many people get into grooves such as thinking that life is unfair to them. They worry, become stressful, afraid, nervous and so on. They develop phobias about being sick, about being discriminated against. They are sure that everyone is against them, and doubt everyone, including their better-half.

There are no quick-fix solutions

If you happen to be the spouse of such a person, what can you do? Plenty! Instead of cribbing about the problem, think about taking professional help. Think about friends and near and dear ones. Talk to them. They can talk to your partner. You can talk to your better-half.

Just as a man is fulfilled through working out the intricate details of solving a problem, a woman is fulfilled through talking about the details of her problems.

You can surely help your spouse to reduce stress and worry. Not overnight. Not in a quarter. Not even in a year! Learn a lesson from the proverbial tortoise who is slower than the hare, but wins the race.

In real life, there are no quick-fix solutions. Therefore, do your research and find out what is worrying your spouse. At this stage, he or she is likely to be more like an onion and, therefore, you will have to peel off the layers, i.e. his or her initial remarks, one by one to get to the heart of the problem. Don't forget, even a lion has to protect himself from the flies and mosquitoes! Your partner may be harbouring silly little doubts or misunderstandings or "what if..." fears. Try to find out patiently what is troubling your better-half. Most probably you will get to the root of his or her problems — in his or her business, job, relationships, other activities — those little matters which your spouse may have magnified many times over.

The solution to your better-half's problems is simple! Encourage and help your partner to take action — bit by bit, again and again. You don't have to be a psychiatrist to help your spouse.

Let me tell you a dramatic incident which shows how sometimes a husband or wife can do what seems impossible, to help his or her better-half.

My cousin Vijay was involved in a very bad road accident. No one stopped to help him. His wife dealt with the situation bravely and stood in front of an oncoming truck. The truck stopped. She 'loaded" her husband onto the truck and saved him.

Whenever you have a problem, think about it 96 per cent of the time. Go 360 degrees to solve it. Talk to people, read books and magazines, write — success will eventually be yours if you have a focused mind. The mightiest tree falls with a humble axe on the hundredth stroke. It does not mean the earlier ninety-nine strokes did not contribute to the success.

Behind every proverbial "overnight" success, there are twenty years of hard work. You can also do small things well and eventually these will make the difference in everything life has to offer.

7 Walk on the same path

Made for each other... to begin with! As we go along in life, small things start getting magnified. Each spouse can ensure that this does not happen, and if it begins to happen, nip it in the bud! An attitude of "KFP" *(kee farak painda* — what difference does it make) to prevent minor problems from becoming major roadblocks to happiness — helps.

> **Each person needs to be loved in his or her own special way. The key to making deposits, therefore, is to understand — and to speak — that person's language of love.**
>
> *Covey*

It is equally important to be successful in marriage than in your job or business. Don't forget, when we are ready to meet our maker, we regret not having been nice to each other.

If you are a husband, has it ever happened that you reach home to find your wife having a severe headache? Concerned about her, you offer to take her to a doctor. And suddenly she starts crying. You do not understand. Well, experience shows that what she needs is not a doctor but more of your time. She wants you to give her flowers, and so on. Why does it happen? All day long she has had to tolerate small irritations from the children and the household chores. She keeps on collecting such "grey stamps" and the minute you come late from your office, she explodes on seemingly small lapses on your part. You as a caring husband, must try and understand what is bothering her. Show empathy. It helps — a lot!

A wife, being a more complete person, should walk 60% towards the goal the health and happiness of the family. Remember the song from *My Fair Lady* about forgetting birthdays and anniversaries? Mark all the birthdays and anniversaries of family members and friends on a calendar or planner. So, if you are a wife, become a good prompter! Become your husband's guardian angel and have fun together instead of creating *kya scene hai* (such a scene)!

> **The secret of love is performing some little act daily to give happiness to your beloved — an act of service, perhaps; a small gift; a word of appreciation, a smile of affection.**
>
> *J. Donald Walters*

Look after your own health as well as the health of your husband and children. Ill health can cause you and your near and dear ones much worry and unhappiness. Join your partner in a brisk walk every morning. Take him to the doctor for regular check-ups. Keep in mind that you are both likely to live long and, therefore, you must plan for your twilight years.

Husbands and wives, after a while, sit on different horses — this is a fact. However, they make life more difficult for themselves if they travel in different directions! Stop all this. Kill your *ahankar* (ego) and run by your partner's side, in your better-half's direction — in the end you will never regret it.

8 Think out of the box

If your partner is too fond of eating

If God has given you a better-half with a voracious appetite, think of the following: Think of the story of the elephant and the six blind men. To the first the side was a wall, to the second the tusk was a spear, to the third the trunk was a snake, to the fourth the leg was a tree, to the fifth the ear was a fan and to the sixth the tail was a rope.

> **God grant me the serenity**
> **To accept the things I cannot change,**
> **The courage to change the things I can,**
> **And the wisdom to know the difference.**

You too can look at your partner with your eyes, ears, nose, head and heart, or you can look at him or her like the proverbial blind men. Don't compare your partner with others. It won't help, but will only make you unhappy. Let your spouse have fun and eat to his or her heart's content. It may not be good, but then your "concern" is ten times more harmful to your better-half's self-esteem and self-respect.

So, don't nag. But take your time to think of creative ways to improve your better-half's eating habits. When you start thinking creatively, you see interrelationships and processes of change rather than snapshots, which will enable you to focus on the roots of the problems and tackle them one by one.

If your spouse smokes like a chimney

With regard to smoking, I am reminded of a saying, *"It does not matter whether you drown in six inches or six or sixty feet of water."*

If your better-half smokes like a chimney, what do you do? Simple. Shift your mind to start thinking out of the box instead of along straight lines. When you say smoking is bad you are thinking in a straight line, and you are getting away from the problem.

I have seen many smokers who are alive and happy and have come across many non-smokers who are more stressful.

Please don't get me wrong. I am not saying smoking is good, I am only saying it is a smaller evil than you think it to be. So, don't overkill! Help your spouse think of simple ways to overcome smoking — gradually.

If your better-half loves the bottle

The mere mention of drinking... and you start thinking of alcoholism! It starts as simple social drinking and because of low self-esteem and work and home-related stresses, it becomes a disease.

Let me tell you an ancient Sufi story.

A passerby encounters a drunk on his hands and knees under a street lamp. He offers to help, and finds out that the drunk is looking for his house keys. After a while, he asks, "Where did you drop them?" The drunk replies that he dropped the keys outside his front door.

"Then why look for them here?" asks the passerby.

"Because," says the drunk, "there is no light by my doorway."

In life, tackle fundamental problems by finding creative solutions. Ignore the obvious solutions. Sometimes the keys are indeed under the street lamp; but very often they are not visible in the darkness. After all, if the solution was easy, it would already have been found. What you need is not the proverbial bigger hammer, but the right hammer.

> **A man wants to make improvements when he feels he is being approached as the solution to a problem rather than as the problem itself.**
>
> *Pease*

Understand that drinking is a bad habit and a debit entry into your better-half's health account. But don't make your spouse feel bad all over and lose his self-esteem.

Be patient with your spouse. Remember, your better-half should be able to feel the need for overcoming the bad habit of drinking, only then can your spouse give up drinking. You can play a very supportive role by making your better-half realise why he must get over the bad habit of drinking.

A friend of mine weighs over 130 kg, drinks, smokes and eats a lot during get-togethers. His ever-smiling wife enjoys the scene from a distance. If ever I have seen a supportive wife, she is one. It has been this way for thirty years. I asked her about it, and her simple reply was, *"Let him have fun. He is grown up enough to understand what is good and what is not good for him and his family."*

Let me tell you an interesting story.

During the American Civil War, some generals complained to Abraham Lincoln that General Grant was very fond of the bottle. Lincoln retorted that he would discuss the topic with them at the meeting to be held the next day. Lincoln was a wise man and took time to think and put himself in the other person's shoes. The next day at the meeting he asked, "Tell me, which brand does General Grant drink? Maybe he wins battles because of this! If that is the case, maybe I should send him a carton of his favourite drink every month!"

So, if your husband is a good provider and a good man, help him to slowly wean himself away from the bottle. Don't create scenes every day! However, if your better-half's problem is unmanageable, take professional help and advice.

9

Become your better-half's cheerleader

Empower your spouse by becoming his or her biggest cheerleader. Help your better-half to develop contacts by networking. You don't have to become a social butterfly but be supportive. In the USA, the Rolodex is the proverbial light bulb. In our country, the visiting cards folder takes its place. The Rolodex is so important in the USA that they say, if your house is on fire, forget your jewellery, your wedding album, but save your Rolodex!

> **One of the best parts of being a family is that you can encourage one another. You can believe in one another. You can affirm one another.**
>
> *Covey*

Keep birthday cards, Diwali cards, New Year cards. Become helpful. Do your homework. Dig your well before you become thirsty. Your visiting cards folder can become your guardian angel whenever you need any help — whether it's regarding a change of job, getting more business, planning a vacation, getting information which may be useful in match-making or anything else. It can become your Ganeshjee's hand! Use it as your *Brahmastra* for networking, interfacing and storing vital information. This *Brahmastra* may not guarantee your better-half's success. But surely it is far better to have it in place should you ever need it. Remember, 96 per cent of your contacts won't be able to help your better-half, but probably you will need only one to make the difference.

In the times ahead in India, your spouse can lose his or her job or business. Motivate your partner to hone his or her skills in addition to networking. Encourage your better-half to exceed targets. Remember, "encourage" don't "nag".

Go along with your spouse. Be a partner in your better- half's dreams. Become your better-half's friend. Make your spouse your world. Don't let inhibitions get in your way. Talk. Walk together. Think. Understand. Reflect. Rationalise. Do your homework to talk to your spouse intelligently. Ask your better-half questions, which will make him or her think. Develop good listening skills. Become your better-half's sounding board. Become your partner's consultant.

The role of parents
is a unique one, a
sacred stewardship
in life. Is there really
anything that would
outweight the importance
of fulfilling that
stewardship well ?

TWO

You and your children

There was a time when parents knew instinctively how to raise their children according to time- honoured traditions. But in today's fast-changing world, values have undergone a sea-change. To groom our children into well-adjusted adults, we as parents need to take a few lessons too! We can inculcate the right values in our children by not only telling them how they can be good, but by showing them how to be good — with our own example.

I may not always be the best father to my children, but I do make every effort I can to be one. As a parent, I am still learning a lot from this thought-provoking saying:

Children have never been very good at listening to their elders, but they have never failed to imitate them.

My research on the parent-child relationship has led me to the conclusion that the 70:30 formula applies to good parenting — 70 per cent effort and 30 per cent pure luck. While by no means denying the importance of luck in the successful future of our children, my experience has been that if we concentrate on hard work and positive actions — the pro-active 70 per cent, chances are that the 30 per cent luck will also turn up trumps.

Life is funny. We get manuals for Maruti, Onida, Yamaha and thousands of other brands, but not one on managing our children! Let me share with you some thought-starters, which are an integral part of the pro-active 70 per cent effort I put in as a parent. They may help you to put together your own children's manual. And, if you succeed, read this "manual" regularly — with your children beside you and a red pencil in your hand. Make your own scrapbook of clippings from newspapers and magazines. Talk with your friends and relatives. Observe. Experiment. Think. Reflect. Custom-build your "manual".

10

Build a bond of love

As a parent your moment of triumph is when your children grow up to be fine human beings. More often than not, we burden our children with the weight of our unrealistic expectations. This touching letter, which W. Livingstone Larned wrote to his son, brings out beautifully how we as parents can often be unfairly demanding even without meaning to be.

Father Forgets

Listen, son: I am saying this as you lie asleep, one little paw crumpled under your cheek and the blond curls stickily wet on your damp forehead. I have stolen into your room alone. Just a few minutes ago, as I sat reading my paper in the library, a stifling wave of remorse swept over me. Guiltily I came to your bedside.

These are the things I was thinking son: I had been cross at you. I scolded you as you were dressing for school because you gave your face merely a dab with a towel. I took you to task for not cleaning your shoes. I called out angrily when you threw some of your things on the floor.

At breakfast I found fault, too. You spilled things. You

gulped down your food. You put your elbows on the table. You spread butter too thick on your bread. And as you started off to play and I made for my train, you turned and waved a hand and called, "Good-bye Daddy! " and I frowned, and said in reply: "Hold your shoulders back! "

Then it began all over again in the late afternoon. As I came up the road I spied you, down on your knees, playing marbles. There were holes in your stockings. I humiliated you before your boy friends by marching you ahead of me to the house. Stockings were expensive — and if you had to buy them you would be more careful. Imagine that, son, from a father!

Do you remember, later, when I was reading in the library, how you came in, timidly, with a sort of hurt look in your eyes? When I glanced up over my paper, impatient at the interruption, you hesitated at the door. "What is it you want?" I snapped.

You said nothing but ran across in one tempestuous plunge, and threw your arms around my neck and kissed me, and your small arms tightened with an affection that God had set blooming in your heart and which even neglect could not wither. And then you were gone, pattering up the stairs.

Well, son, it was shortly afterwards that my paper slipped from my hands and a terrible sickening fear came over me. What has habit been doing to me? The habit of finding fault, of reprimanding — this was my reward to you for being a boy. It was not that I did not love you; it was that I expected too much of you. I was measuring you by the yardstick of my own years.

And there was so much that was good and fine and true in your character. The little heart of yours was as big as the dawn itself over the wide hills. This is shown by your spontaneous impulse to rush in and kiss me good-night. Nothing else matters tonight, son. I have come to your bedside in darkness, and I have knelt there, ashamed!

It is feeble atonement; I know you would not understand these things if I told them to you during your waking hours. But tomorrow I will be a real daddy! I will chum with you, and suffer when you suffer, and laugh when you laugh. I will bite my tongue when impatient words come. I will keep saying as if it were a ritual: "He is nothing but a boy — a little boy!"

I am afraid I have visualised you as a man. Yet as I see you now, son, crumpled and weary in your cot, I see that you are still a baby. Yesterday, you were in your mother's arms, your head on her shoulder. I have asked too much, too much.

Managing children, since the days of the *Ramayana* and *Mahabharata,* has always been an impossible job. The challenge lies in making the impossible as beautiful as possible. There are no simple equations — there is no science. Raising children is purely an art, which with practice and patience one can hope to master.

Parents learn a lot from their children about coping with life.

Parents should get the credits and debits for what their children turn out to be as they have a great role to play in conditioning their children. This requires tremendous amounts of self-control and patience, and also the wisdom to do things that might seem disciplinarian but are, in fact, necessary.

Children are assets but, if parents do not nurture and encourage them, they are likely to become liabilities. It is as simple as that! So, to be able to manage their children, parents must first be able to manage themselves.

As a parent, I have learnt a lot from the following incident of World War II. It was a few years after the reverses of the American Navy at Pearl Harbour. The new fleet was sent to the Pacific to confront the Japanese and the Admiral in charge was relaxing in the officers' mess. He was asked by the reporters how he was so relaxed when his men were at sea, engaged in a severe sea-battle.

The Admiral replied calmly: "Gentlemen, to the best of my abilities, I trained my men, equipped them and briefed them. I have done the best I could. Now, as my men are at sea, there is nothing I can do, so why should I worry and become stressful."

The way you fulfill your monitoring role will have a profound effect on your child's sense of self-worth and on your ability to influence and teach.

Children too are like ships and once they venture out into the world, they will have to fend for themselves. We can't be with them always. So, while they are with us let us give them the best education. Let us do nothing of which they may be ashamed. Let us share with them what we read, write, think or do. Let us respect our elders so that they will do the same. Remember, they are watching us — just as God is watching us from above. Of course we make mistakes, sometimes very small ones and occasionally big ones. But let us always be ready to say sorry — with words as well as deeds.

We should not worry if we cannot give them what other parents can — such as vacations in Goa or Kashmir or chauffeur-driven BMWs to take them to school or college. But we should be there to comfort them when they get hurt or when they are feeling low. We should make sure that they get the best smiles life can offer and should be there to hold them — if they stumble. When there are tears, they should have the confidence that we will be there to wipe them away.

11

Walk 13 steps with your children

My observations on the parent-children relationship have brought me to the conclusion that parents must put themselves in their children's shoes — every time, every day! Have you ever complained to yourself that your children do not understand you? Next time you think that way, imagine your children saying the same to themselves about you. There is undoubtedly a communication gap between the two of you, and you must do everything you can to bridge it.

> **When you understand you don't judge.**
>
> *Covey*

Raising children is one of the most important and difficult jobs parents will ever have. It's a job all parents accept even though they usually have very little experience and absolutely no formal training.

After thirty years of observing, experiencing, reading and discussing the subject of raising children and countless brainstorming sessions with parents, I have come up with an update, a snap study, call it what you want, on *How To Raise Children.* All the steps mentioned here are simple ways, which you can start putting into practice from today. Remember, it is never too late to start conditioning your children towards becoming good for everything.

The 8 Steps For You

Inculcate the right values in your children by making efforts towards becoming a good parent. I have come up with eight simple steps which we as parents need to take.

STEP 1

Learn the art of story-telling

Good stories can help your children cultivate a positive attitude to life, and can also help them to make more friends. Stories, especially short ones like the tales from the Panchatantra, are the best thought-starters in the world, and can act as warning signals for your children whenever they are in danger of getting derailed. Perhaps just a hundred will do: but keep repeating these in their growing-up years.Fables like the one about the Thirsty Crow, or The Lion and The Mouse will teach them far more and do greater wonders for them in their early years than most college degrees can do later in life.

> **To talk to a child, to fascinate him, is much more difficult than to win an electoral victory. But it is also more rewarding.**
>
> *Colette*

STEP 2

Be their friend

Remove your children's "what-if" fears by assuring them that whenever they are in trouble or doubt, you will be there to help them. You will not laugh at their silly doubts or stupid thoughts and will be there to straighten out their thinking. They can have a good sounding-board in you.

> **There is no friendship, no love, like that of the parent for the child.**

Tell them to come to you whenever they want and with whatever mistake they have made, and assure them that you will listen to them before judging them and will assist them accordingly. Tell them that they are your children and will remain so irrespective of whatever happens to them in life — whether they become a peon or a president, the poorest of the poor or the richest of the rich. Your confidence in them is very essential.

STEP 3

Put yourself in their shoes

Do not compare your children's situation with your own which existed a quarter of a century ago when you were their age. Things have changed. You had a reverence for your parents, which was the result of the social environment at that time; you did not reason; you accepted their word without a question.

> **Don't judge a child until you have walked in his moccasins.**

Remember, your children are the products of today's environment, of the "information explosion". Your children are now more confused than you were about social values. Be patient with them. They are intelligent. Compared to your fifty summers, their twenty-five summers have given them a depth and breadth of knowledge, which you did not possess at that age.

To be a good parent, you have to put yourself in their shoes, and to recognise that your children have feelings and needs which are different from yours. Never expect gratitude from your children, and in case you get it, be pleasantly surprised. Your children think whatever material things you give them is their birthright — since their childhood they have been brainwashed into believing this. You are doing for your children what your father did for you — this has been happening since times immemorial and is likely to continue forever.

When I was young I wanted a bicycle and I was very happy when my father bought me one. My son naturally expected a Rajdoot from me, but never got one! I convinced him that, it would be better if he finished college, and then went in for the best buy. He was wise enough to sacrifice his today for tomorrow and the result is that, today, he owns a Honda Accord.

STEP 4

Give them your time

Spend time with your children. Play games with them, read to them, help them with their homework, ask them about their friends. Talk less; listen more. Let them open their hearts to you.

Sometimes, children have an awkward relationship

with their fathers. They usually enjoy an easy, relaxed relationship with their mothers but have a difficult time communicating with their fathers. But times are changing. Nowadays, fathers play an equally important role in bringing up their children.

If you are a father, make sure that you have two-way communication with your children. It is hard to accomplish but not impossible. Let them have the confidence that you will be there when they need you. There are certain aspects of life that they would like to talk over with you, and not with their mother. Be there for them on such vital occasions.

If you want your children to turn out well, spend twice as much time with them and half as much money on them.

While communicating with your children, be aware that silence often works better than words. Lend a patient ear to them. Perhaps, there are times when they just want to share their innermost thoughts with you.

I used to drive my daughter to her tuition classes every sunday. It took me an hour to reach her to her destination. Giving her my most precious asset – time, helped me understand her better. I let her know that it was a pleasure for me to spend Sunday mornings with her, instead of grumbling about how it was spoiling my holiday!

Try being there for your children when they need you. Let your children get the feeling that their parents not only love them but that they also *care* for them.

Don't be parents who provide everything to their children — TV, VCR, Hi Fi — everything except their time.

Take time off from your busy routine and spend it with your children. They need your undivided attention more than anyone else. Children "see-through" when parents make a sacrifice for them and never forget it. In the final analysis, those parents who "bleed" more, are more satisfied with their children. Learn to bleed for your children. Do not merely finance them.

STEP 5

Do not criticise them

Do not criticise your children, especially in front of others. Shouting at or beating them will make them feel small, confused and hurt, and they will become more stubborn. Try to reason with them in a calm manner. If you find yourself getting angry, do not shout. Give them time to work things out for themselves.

> **Praise your children openly, reprove them secretly.**
> *W.Cecil*

Never expect the impossible from them by having your unrealistic expectations. Children are more in need of example than of criticism. Some children flower at 10... some at 20... some at 30! Don't be impatient. Above all, don't compare your children with other children. Comparisons are odious and will make your children lose confidence in themselves.

STEP 6

Set a good example

As your children grow up they will develop their own self-correcting devices, which evolve naturally through education, training and exposure — and most of all from observing you. So, whatever you want your children to be, become that yourself first. In your thoughts, words, actions and emotional responses.

Just as the roots of the tree bring nutrients and life to every other parts of the tree, so your own example gives life to your relationships, to your efforts to organize, to your opportunities to teach.

Your children are copy-cats and their mental antennae are always tuned in to your signals. They observe you very closely. Don't let their years fool you. They are definitely more "tuned" to you than you can imagine. Inculcate the values of honesty, loyalty, sincerity, good manners and politeness in them.

Teach your children self-restraint by practising it yourself. Don't try to explain things by shouting at them when they are wrong, but by setting an example of what is right. Remember, anger is an expensive luxury, which only people of tremendous means can afford. It is a sign of faulty development in a person. Avoid it yourself. Do not get angry when the servant puts an extra spoonful of sugar in your tea. Is it worth getting angry about? Still, many people do exactly that. Children who grow up watching their mother or father scream at the servant or throw things about in a fit of rage, will do the same when they grow up.

Set an example for your children by not making an avoidable phone call or pulling up an errant cabbie for over-charging you. Try being as honest, truthful and sincere as possible. Your children may poke fun at you, but eventually they will be very proud of you.

Once, Akbar the Great was presented with a bottle of exotic perfume. While applying it, a drop fell on the floor. He bent down instantly and rubbed the spot with his fingers. He realized, only too late, that Birbal had been observing him with rapt attention. The next day, an embarrassed Akbar proclaimed in his Durbar *that all the fountains in the palace would be filled with the rare perfume for six days.*

However, Birbal did not appear impressed with Akbar's generosity and whispered into the emperor's ears, "Boond se gayee izzat, hauz se nahin aatee!" *(The respect lost in a drop cannot be regained with reservoirs.)*

General Douglas MacArthur had the following put up in his room.

Build Me A Son...

Build me a son, O Lord, who will be strong enough to face himself when he is afraid; one who will be proud and unbending in honest defeat, and humble and gentle in victory.

Lead him, O Lord, not in the path of ease and comfort but under the stress and spur of difficulties and challenges.

Here let him learn to stand up to the storm; here let him learn compassion for those who fail.

Build me a son whose heart will be clear; whose goal will be high... One who will reach for the future, yet never forget the past.

Give him humility, so that he may always remember the simplicity of true greatness, the open mind of true wisdom and the meekness of true strength.

Then, I, his father, will dare to whisper: "I have not lived in vain."

STEP 7

Respect your spouse

Don't nag your better-half, especially in front of your children. And even if you find that you tend to do so, confess privately to your children that you are ashamed of the habit and are trying to get rid of it. Admitting your mistakes makes both you and your children wiser. Try it.

> **The greatest thing you can do for your children is — respect your spouse.**
>
> *Covey*

Nagging is the result of muddled-up thinking, wrong priorities and mental mess-up. It is due to your habit of magnifying small things into big things. Then a "mouse" of a problem becomes a monster!

Respect for your spouse is very important if you want to bring up your children well. I have found a simple way to respect my wife. I have made a list of her good habits and practices. Of course she had many bad habits and practices which "emerged" after a few years of marriage. However, I became wiser and started appreciating her good habits. I have also realised that I do not have to wait for her to do great things before I respect her, I can start respecting her by looking for small things, which she does well.

My daughters respect me for not nagging my wife. They also respect their mother because I respect her. Silence. Patience. Managing anger. Not shouting. And maintaining an attitude of KFP — *kee farak painda* (what difference does it make) — in regard to whatever she does has made all the difference in my life.

STEP 8

Have good friends

Keep good company for your children's sake. You cannot choose your relatives but you can always choose friends. And you need not have hundreds of them; less than a dozen will do. Your children will observe your friends very closely — both consciously and subconsciously. They will form their own opinions of each of your friends. Let them use their judgement as to what they want to soak in or filter out. In their minds, there is a huge sponge, eager to absorb new experiences.

My son observed one of my friends very carefully and learnt to be humble, hard working and humorous. Perhaps the best quality he picked up from my buddy is the ability to laugh at himself.

The 5 Steps For Them

Your role as a parent is incomplete unless you take pains to teach your children some essential coping skills. Let's talk about five easy steps, which you can take as a good parent to make your children better human beings.

STEP 1

Teach them to be responsible

Life is all about making and taking decisions — when we should get up, what to wear, what to eat and so on. Many of us, when we overprotect our children, are in fact harming them. Parents have to take a decision as to when and how much freedom or money to give their children. There is no one way or easy way. It has to be seen in totality.

> **The most important thing that parents can teach their childen is how to get along without them.**
>
> *Frank A. Clark*

Teach your children to be responsible persons. Teach them not to be ashamed of carrying out any task assigned to them. From the time they are young, assign little tasks to them. Encourage them to keep their books and toys in the proper place. When they finish their projects they must tidy up, and not leave others to clear up the mess after them.

Send your children, when they are big enough, on small errands outside the house. Expose your children to the realities of life, such as going to the bank, paying electricity, bills, posting letters. They will grow up, mentally — very fast!

If you help them in making and taking decisions they are likely to make wiser and better decisions later on. These decisions will at first be very small impact-wise, but making decisions, which have bigger impacts in terms of money, time, respect and happiness is what life has in store for them.

Learn to mix equal doses of affection and discipline when you are bringing up your children. Protect them from harm but do not mollycoddle them. By being over-protective you might be blocking their vision. Let them become independent.

Parenting is not about being popular and giving in to every child's whim and desire. It's about making decisions that truly are win-win — however they may appear to the child at the time.

You want to give your children all the good things in life. But there are times when you can't. Learn to say no to your children when it is necessary. Very often, a clear and distinct no can save a hundred heartaches! Parents who don't teach their children their duties are as guilty as the children who neglect them in their old age.

Between birth and the eighth year children must learn to understand love, discipline, respect, courtesy, and accommodation. If parents can teach these during the first 100 months of their children's life, they can anticipate greater odds in their favour for the future.

In the next 100 months, children should learn the meaning of money. This major lesson in economics is probably best taught between the ages of 8 and 16. Expecting your children to understand money before they are eight is meaningless and telling them how to handle cash after they are sixteen probably won't make much difference.

You can teach your children their responsibilities by becoming more innovative and objective, and most importantly, by your own example. Remember that your children have a video-cassette recorder in their mind which is not only recording your voice — when you tell fibs on the phone, for instance — but your eye and body movements also. The way you treat your better-half, your parents, colleagues and employees — all this is getting recorded to be played back to you later!

As your children grow up to be adults, they develop complexes and, to express themselves, they might develop expensive tastes — fast cars, flashy clothes! Why is it so? Think. Maybe you can give them more responsibility. Try to steer them away from negative influences — but don't dictate what they should do. That will only isolate them — let them learn from their own mistakes, and overlook some of them.

STEP 2

Teach them to learn to lose and to enjoy winning

Encourage your children to take active part in games and sports. Train them like a coach trains a star athlete. Teach them to be courteous winners and sporting losers. This attitude will go a long way in preparing them to meet the challenges of life head on.

Abraham Lincoln wrote a letter to his son's teacher. It is a timeless classic. Here is an extract.

Teach My Son...

...He will have to learn, I know, that all men are not just, all men are not true. But teach him also that for every scoundrel there is a hero; that for every selfish politician, there is a dedicated leader.

Teach him that for every enemy there is a friend. It will take time, I know, but teach him if you can, that a dollar earned is of far more value than five found.

Teach him to learn to lose and also to enjoy winning. Steer him away from envy, if you can, teach him the secret of quiet laughter. Let him learn early that bullies are the easiest to lick.

Teach him, if you can, the wonder of books but also give him quite some time to ponder the eternal mystery of birds in the sky, bees in the sun, and flowers on a green hillside.

In school teach him that it is far more honourable to fail than to cheat. Teach him to have faith in his own ideas, even if everyone tells him they are wrong.

Teach him to be gentle with gentle people, and tough with the tough. Try to give my son the strength not to follow the crowd when everyone is getting on the band-wagon. Teach him to listen to all men but teach him also to filter all he hears on a screen of truth and take only the good that comes through.

Teach him, if you can, how to laugh when he is sad. Teach him there is no shame in tears. Teach him to scoff at cynics and beware of too much sweetness.

Teach him to sell his brawn and brain to the highest bidders, but never to put a price tag on his heart and soul. Teach him to close his ears to the howling mob and to stand up and fight if he thinks he is right.

Teach him gently, but do not coddle fine steel. Let him have the courage to be impatient, let him have the patience to be brave. Teach him always to have sublime faith in mankind.

This is a big order, but see what you can do. He is such a fine little fellow, my son.

STEP 3

Give them the best education

Recently one of my colleagues had a brainstorming session with me about his daughter who had just completed her schooling. He was thinking out loud about sending her for computer education, expecting that within two or three years she would get a job paying her Rs. 12,000 to Rs. 15,000 per month, and in the process save three years of college too.

To me this was like taking the fun out of life. Skipping campus life may be the smart thing to do, but it is certainly not a wise thing. I really do not know why we want our children to grow up so fast that they always regret it when they look back. Some parents send their two-year-old children to school, and make their simple lives complex.

Education is an ornament of prosperity. Give your children the best education that money and love can buy. No one can take that away from them — ever!

When my younger daughter was eight and studying in the third standard, I once found her muttering to herself, "Papa is lucky. He comes home, drinks tea, watches TV, reads magazines, has his dinner, goes to sleep and he has no worries. Look at me! I have to do my homework, prepare my bag for the next day, and I am always afraid of my teachers and my mother as I have to get good marks."

A dealer friend of mine once mentioned: "One evening when I reached home, I found my daughter-in-law scolding my granddaughter, with whom I had been looking forward to playing with her on reaching home, for getting 85% marks *instead of 95%.*"

To me, education means that your children can play with their grandparents, parents, uncles, aunts, and friends. I would rather see my children get 60% marks and hear their happy laughter every evening than have them become sullen bookworms who score 95%.

Let your children choose their own profession — whether it is medicine, computer science, dress designing, or catering. Encourage them to develop a passion for reading, music, sports, or whatever interests them. Arrange for them to see good movies and plays, to visit exhibitions and art galleries, to go trekking and camping with school groups. They will emerge as happier and more complete persons.

STEP 4

Let them grow

Expose your children to as many situations as you can. Let them go on excursions with friends, learn swimming, go rock-climbing and river-rafting, join the National Cadet Corps and social work groups in school and college.

No matter which profession you are in, don't push your children into it if they are reluctant. A frame can define or limit your children's potential. Provide your children with the necessary paints and brushes but let them find a canvas that fits their personalities.

Many parents hang on to their children for too long and then it becomes too late. Don't tie your children to your apron-strings. Let them pursue whatever they are interested in — medicine, publishing, catering, engineering, law, fine arts, farming, or running a business.

Raja Dasharatha sent his four sons to the Gurukul. It was very difficult for him, but he knew he had to do it. You too have a very vital role to play as a parent. Motivate your children. Help them make their dreams come true by encouraging them to work towards their goals.

Your children are like uncut diamonds. Smoothen out their rough edges patiently and with expertise. Patiently, because as the Chinese proverb says, *"with time the mulberry leaf becomes silk."* If your children grow up to be fine, well-adjusted human beings, it means you have been successful as a parent. So, expose your children to new and interesting situations... and watch them grow up to be good and mature adults.

Your child is like a book, which you can't read when it's too close or too distant.

Help your children to become worldly-wise. Tell them about the "third eye" of Lord Shiva. Help them to understand people better. They cannot learn this in any school or college, but only from you and from books. Share your observations with them and give them books, which will help them analyse things in the right perspective.

Let them talk to your friends, professionals, bankers, government officials, and absorb different experiences. If possible, let them spend a few days in a joint-family system, a few days in a family where both husband and wife work, a few days in a big city, a few days in a small town, and a few days on a farm or in a village.

Teach your children the ABCs of running a house.

Let them be involved in the annual repairs of the house. A very successful father I know gave his children a cheque book of their own at 12 years of age and deposited in their accounts the sums spent on their behalf for lessons, doctors' fees, education, books, trips, clothes, etc. Fifteen years later his children were far better money managers than their contemporaries who were never exposed to handling money.

> **Let your children go if you want to keep them.**
> *Malcolm Forbes*

Groom your children to be confident and caring hosts. Once in a while let them treat their friends in style. Suggest that they should have good and trustworthy friends. Make sure that your children attend family get-togethers, funerals, and marriages; encourage them to do things and get involved in such rituals. Dispel their fears. Keep an eye on them from a distance but do not pester them or fuss over them. Let them develop their own style. Your children are never too young to do things. Have you seen ten-year-old boys driving *tongas* on busy roads? Akbar became the emperor of India when he was thirteen!

God has fitted the world's largest computer in your children's mind with a screen of 90m x 90m with over a million hooks on it. This "3-in-l" system enables him to soak in every idea you expose him to, and which he carefully pegs on each hook. All your children need is opportunities to widen their horizons, which only you can give them.

STEP 5

Encourage them to read

Read to your children from the time they are very young. You will be surprised how much they will absorb. Soon they will start reading on their own. Provide them with good and interesting books. Talk to them about what they are reading. Discuss with them the merits and demerits of books you and they have read. Reading good books is a habit that always pays off. Inculcate the habit of reading in your children from their formative years.

A house without books is like a room without windows. No man has a right to bring up his children without surrounding them with books, if he has the means to buy them. Children learn to read by being in the presence of books. The love of knowledge comes with reading and grows upon it. And the love of knowledge, in a young mind, is almost a warrant against the inferior excitement of passions and vices.

Horace Mann

A family business is not a gift. It is a challenge. It is an opportunity. It is a commitment and dedication to the belief that something worthwhile can be built.

THREE

Make your family business a dream come true

There are no hard and fast rules, no best ways, which the head of a family business can adopt to make the business a successs. Most often, the new business owner goes from the Wonder Stage, when he wonders what in hell he's supposed to do, through a Blunder Stage where his hard work makes up for his mistakes. Following Blunder is usually Thunder, the time of the increasingly successful, and sometimes obnoxiously successful business owner. The fourth and final stage has two labels — Plunder or Rebirth of Wonder — depending on how well the founder plans for the future.

For all the decisions — good or bad — taken by him, his successors have to face the music! They inherit the restrictions, the frustrations and the deficiencies linked to the business; at the same time, they inherit the strengths and opportunities attached to it — it is a package deal of "plus" and "minus" factors. The successors cannot bring back the founder nor can they applaud him for the plus points or beat him up for the minus points which were his doing.

So, what does one who is steering the family business do? The least he can do is — draw inspiration from what I call, the Twelve Commandments, to tackle the ups and downs of the business.

I am not saying that these commandments can be a panacea to all the problems in a family business. But, they will certainly compel the business owner to communicate with his family members and move in the right direction. Without this communication, the business owner and his family are on different horses, riding off into separate sunsets, while the business stumbles along like a mule with blinders — tunnel-visioned and sterile.

Twelve commandments for the business owner

1. *I will share my dreams with my family.*
2. *I will inform my managers and employees, "This company will continue forever."*
3. *I will develop a workable organisation and make it visible on a chart.*
4. *I will do all I can to improve the managerial skills of my managers, my family and myself.*
5. *I will put a functional accounting system in place, which will make relevant data available to managers, advisors, and directors.*
6. *I will develop a council of competent advisors.*
7. *I will ask a board of competent outside directors to review the business.*
8. *I will choose my successor(s).*
9. *I will groom my successor (s) to step into my shoes.*
10. *I will retire and install my successor(s) with my powers within my lifetime.*
11. *I will settle my estate plans as I cannot take my material possessions with me when I leave for my heavenly adobe.*
12. *I will leave no stone unturned in abidind by the above commondments.*

12

Groom your Loved ones

The failure to teach, or the reluctance to learn are two of the biggest mistakes in a family business. As early as possible, in terms and words that will be understandable to their children, father and mothers should seek to share the dream of the family busines – the things it does, the people involved, the markets served, the satisfactions realised, the stories of the past, and the hopes for the future.

> **We make a living by what we get, but we make a life by what we give.**
>
> *Norman MacEswan*

Dr. Leon Danco, author of *Inside the Family Business* and Head of The Center for family Business, University Services Institute, in Cleveland, Ohio says:

> *Children are not born with an understanding of what they can do or what they are worth to others. They surely won't have any idea what the world expects of them unless we make sure that they find out. And they'll find this out best in the hands of objective outsiders. If at all possible we should try to postpone bringing our heirs right away into the family business — they deserve a chance to learn about themselves on their own by getting their first jobs from somebody else. There are two significant benefits to this. First, it will*

allow the young man or woman the opportunity to collect credentials in the eyes of the non-family employees. Second, working for somebody else can develop a powerful appreciation for the benefits and value of the family business.

The business owner — or more likely, his tax advisors — can come up with all kinds of tax reasons for overpaying our kids for minimal work they never did. But saving on taxes or beating Uncle Sam out of his share (deserved and undeserved) is no reason to ruin our children. It's almost an unwritten law: cheat the tax collector and spoil the child.

For the business founder, the duty to groom his loved ones, increases with every passing year, but that duty doesn't necessarily bring with it the ability to teach well. A true teacher plants seeds in what he hopes is fertile soil, seeds which then sprout and grow in their own way with only as much of his help as is absolutely necessary.

> **Education does not take place when you learn something you did not know before. Education is your ability to use what you have learned to be better today than you were yesterday.**
>
> *Iyanla Vanzant*

As a businessman you may have started the enterprise as a doer. But as a father, in all likelihood, you may not be a good teacher or a trainer if you are short tempered, cannot stand questions and objections from your children, and are impatient. So, what is the solution?

One way you could deal with the situation is to

expose your children to situations where they will be forced to learn. You could also ask your friends and colleagues — whose opinions you value, to guide them. You could also send your children to work for your business friends or you could let them find meaningful jobs for themselves. Such experiences will teach your children a lot.

So, don't get into a groove with the *mera bachcha* (my poor child!) feeling. It takes away the joy of learning from our children. Remember, a cub becomes a lion when he makes his own kill. What your children will learn in two years in another organisation cannot be learnt by them in your set-up in as much as six years.

Teach them the intricacies of your family business in your own imaginative way, not forgetting that maybe your children can learn more from a visit to a village fair than by going to Harvard Business School! Educate your children creatively. Don't force the family business upon them. Remember, "Education is the only thing lying around loose in the world, and it is the only thing a fellow can have as much of as he is willing to haul away."

Teach them business accountancy

One of the best management education tools available to a business owner is an accounting system that is tailored specifically for the business. Accounting is the only language through which a business can be understood, discussed and defined with any objectivity and accuracy.

A family business owner can use the tool of accounting

as a "language" to teach his children the complexities of the business. If you are grooming your son to be your successor, it will help if you give him business accounting lessons in a creative manner. He does not have to become a financial whizkid, but he should understand figures and the decision making associated with them.

> **Teaching moments are some of the supreme moments of family life — those incomparable times when you know you've made a significant difference in the life of another family member.**
>
> *Covey*

Let me narrate the experience of Dhananjay Vadnagare, the Escorts dealer in Nashik. He joined his father's business as a partner in 1973 but continued with his engineering course at Delhi. His father's time was divided between business, social activities and politics. After completing his studies, he started devoting time to the family business under the "expert" guidance of the business manager. Dhananjay knew nothing of accounts, finance and office management and as he started learning, he discovered the misdeeds of his manager who had, since 1973, neither closed the books of accounts nor filed the income tax and sales tax returns.

Dhananjay did not understand the seriousness of the situation till he was summoned by the income tax officer. He explained the situation to the officer who not only took a sympathetic view of the situation, but also taught him the ABCs of accounting and book keeping. The manager was sacked, books were completed, returns were filed with heavy penalties. However, to control the situation, a department-wise profitability analysis was done and some bold decisions taken. Today Dhananjay is a good dealer of motorcycles. Had Dhananjay received training in business accounts, he would have handled the situation better.

Make them learn things the hard way

The following historic quotation hung for years in the private office of General, Douglas MacArthur, Supreme Commander, Allied Powers, at his General Headquarters in the Dai Ichi Building, Tokyo.

Come with me to Macedonia

Commanders should be counselled chiefly by persons of known talent; by those who have made the art of war their particular study, and whose knowledge is derived from experience; by those who are present at the scene of action, who see the enemy, who see the advantages that occasions offer, and who, like people embarked on the same ship, are sharers of the danger; if therefore, anyone thinks himself qualified to give advice regarding the war which I am to conduct, let him not refuse assistance to the state... but come with me to Macedonia.

He shall be furnished with a ship, a horse, a tent; even his travelling charges shall be defrayed. But if he thinks this too much trouble and prefers the repose of the city life to the toils of war, let him not on land assume the office of pilot.

The city in itself furnishes an abundance of topics for conversation; let it confine its passion for talking to its own precincts and rest assured that we shall pay no attention to any counsel but such as shall be framed within our camp.

—Lucius Aemilius Paulus Roman, Consul Rome, 168 BC.

Let your successors too have a taste of the "battle-field" of business. You should talk to them like Lord Krishna did to Arjuna on the battlefield of Kurukshetra. Instead of confining them to situations where they can only hear the humming of airconditioners, let them hear the road and field noises. Ensure that they travel with you, not in luxury but in harsh conditions. It may sound a bit difficult to implement but it is not impossible.

Chart out plans

Leon A. Danco, in his book *Inside the Family Business,* writes:

If you want to plan for a year, plant corn;
If you want to plan for three years, plant a tree;
But if you want to plan for ten years, plant men!

Fifteen years ago, I got the bright idea to plant some willows on my property. I looked out into my backyard from my den and thought, "Wouldn't two of them be just right, there and over there?"

I went out and bought two saplings about three feet tall and planted them in carefully chosen spots about

20 feet apart. For the next 10 years they grew like only willows can grow. They looked beautiful. I watched, happy and contented from my favourite chair until what should have been obvious became obvious — the trees were starting to overlap and they were only half grown.

I got a book on trees and looked up how large willows can get. I saw that within 20 years they would expand to over 30 foot in diameter. My amateur landscaping plan was no good because I didn't take the time to think about the future.

This sort of problem is very common in family business, only instead of willow trees, we grow family trees. Instead of branches, we deal with stock. There are many stock distribution plans that look very clever today, and they are proposed by people who are experts — the lawyers, accountants and officials who have spent their professional lives getting to know the vast intricacies of the tax laws. But too often instead of taking their advice as just technical advice, business founders tend to ignore their own judgement and follow the prescriptions of the professional 'Rasputins' uncritically and with great eagerness.

I do not want to discourage you and to make you think of inventing various ways of worrying, but then this sort of planning is important in family business too. You have to give about six per cent of your time to this aspect of business.

Organise family meetings

A family meeting with an agenda is a very good management tool for grooming your loved ones. However, the emphasis on the "agenda" should not be undermined. Meetings without agendas are directionless and a sheer waste of time for everyone. The meeting should be as formal as possible and maybe at a different place (possibly in a different town) every time. Weekends are normally congenial for such meetings. Family business is a serious business. Its review and planning for the future cannot be done merely over lunch or dinner.

For such family meetings the size of the business is immaterial. Even if a family business is small, the father, mother, son and daughter can meet once in two or three months — but with an agenda and away from the place of business.

> **Let us make a point, that we meet each other with a smile, when it is difficult to smile. Smile at each other, make time for each other in your family.**
>
> *Mother Teresa*

Family meetings can have the following on the agenda:

1. *Planning for the next month, next year, next five years, next decade.*
2. *Consensus areas where everyone has the same point of view.*

3. *Review of accounts.*
4. *Discussion on family disputes and disagreements.*
5. *Increasing the awareness of the family business — policies, procedures, people, products, and so on.*
6. *Taking and making business decisions.*

Casual conversations always run the risk of becoming "steam valves". See to it that these family meetings, which play a very important role in developing good listening skills, start on time. This is a part of teaching discipline to your would-be successors.

13

Lead your kith and kin like a mentor

Years ago, I saw a movie *Elephant Walk* in which a very successful and well known rancher forced his six-year-old-son to learn horse riding because he mistakenly believed that in order to become like him, his son had to learn to become a good and daring horse rider. The son became afraid of the horse and revolted. Yet the father forced his son to learn horse-riding. The son became extremely nervous. This lone incident changed the personality of the son, and he ended up being a teacher rather than a rancher.

My father too wanted me to become an engineer like him. But I was not good in science and mathematics. A wise man, my father accepted me as I was, and let me proceed at my own pace and in my own direction in life. Had he forced me into becoming an engineer, it is quite possible that I would have become one, but would have been unhappy and unsuccessful in my career.

In a family business too, the best way you can lead your kith and kin is by being their mentor, instead of forcing them to adapt to your ways of handling the business.

J. Willard Marriot (founder of the Marriot Hotel chain in the USA) wrote a letter to his son when he designated him to take over his business. I think these ideas are applicable anywhere... whenever you plan to retire!

Dear Bill,

I am mighty proud of you. Years of preparation, work and study have shown results.

A leader should have character, be an example in all things. This is his greatest influence. In this you are admirable. You have not taken advantage of your position as my son. You remain humble.

You have proved you can manage people and get them to work for you. You have made a profit — your thinker works. You are developing more patience and understanding with people, more maturity.

It is not often a father has a son who can step into his shoes and wear them on the basis of his own accomplishments and ability. Being the operating manager of a business on which probably 30,000 people depend for a livelihood is a frightening responsibility, but I have the greatest confidence you will build a team that will ensure the continued success of a business that has been born through years of toil and devotion by many wonderful people. I have written down a few guideposts — all born out of my experience and ones I wish I could have followed more closely.

Love and best wishes,

Sincerely,

Dad

Guideposts for leading your business to success

Bill's "guideposts" were written on separate sheets of stationery. There were fifteen of them:

1. Keep physically fit, mentally and spiritually strong.
2. Guard your habits — bad ones will destroy you.
3. Pray about every difficult problem.
4. Study and follow professional management principles. Apply them logically and practically to your organisation.
5. Your people are your first priority — their development, loyalty, interest, team spirit are vital. Develop managers in every area. This is your prime responsibility.
6. Decisions: Men grow making decisions and assuming responsibility for them. Make crystal clear what decisions each manager is responsible for and what decisions you reserve for yourself.
7. Criticism: Don't criticise people but make a fair appraisal of their qualifications with their supervisor only (or someone assigned to do this). Remember, anything you say about someone may (and usually does) get back to them. There are few secrets.
8. See the good in people and try to develop those qualities.
9. If inefficiency cannot be overcome and an employee is obviously incapable of the job, find a job he can do or terminate now. Don't wait.

10. Manage your time.

a. Keep your communication short — to the point.

b. Make every minute on the job count.

c. Work fewer hours — some of us waste half our time.

11. Delegate and hold people accountable for results.

12. Details:

a. Let your staff take care of them.

b. Save your energy for planning, thinking, working with department heads and promoting new ideas.

c. Don't do anything someone else can do for you.

13. Ideas and competition:

a. Ideas keep the business alive.

b. Know what your competitors are doing and planning.

c. Encourage your people to think about better ways and give suggestions on anything that will improve business.

14. Don't try to do an employee's job for him — counsel and suggest.

15. Think objectively and keep a sense of humour. Make the business fun for you and others.

(Courtesy: Marriot *by Robert O'Brien*).

14

Keep your mental antennae alert

Ganeshjee, with his big ears, inspires us to listen. People talk, maybe too much, but that is why we have two ears. Listen to everything and filter out whatever is not conducive to helping you.

> **Thoughts, when properly nourished and internalized, will become a reality in your world of form. Thoughts are extremely powerful things.**
>
> *Dr. Wayne Dyer*

When I say *"Learn by listening; understand by reflecting,"* what I mean is, you should not forget to reflect after listening. Ganeshjee's big forehead that stores his big brain is meant for reflecting. Your brain (or mind) can reflect on a thousand things at the same time. For good reflections, learn to relax. While relaxing and reflecting, keep on repeating your thoughts. Never be in a hurry. Take all the time to think and to reflect because your family business is very vital for your "dynasty".

Observe minutely with your eyes what is going on around you. Incidentally, Henry Ford was possibly the most successful industrialist in the world. But when it came to crowning his son, he was a miserable failure. He did not listen. He did not go for counsel. Ultimately, his wife threatened to go back to her parents unless he chose his grandson, Henry Ford II as his successor. Thankfully, he relented and this decision proved to be a boon for the family business.

Many similar stories (rather, real life examples) could be narrated here, but if you just look around in your town, however, small it may be, you will be able to pick them up by the dozen. Remember, you can learn more from a humble leaf than from 100 books.

The small mouth of Ganeshjee reminds us that we should speak less and whenever we speak about something not known to us, we should not hesitate to ask questions even though they may sound foolish! The long nose of Lord Ganeshjee inspires us to poke our nose around, not as an irritant but as a sniffer, to know about the successions in the family businesses of our friends and acquaintances. Ask them about their plans and strategies. It is quite possible that in the process you may be helping your business friends who might not have even started thinking about business succession.

> **Advance confidently in the direction of your own dreams to live the life that you have imagined. That's when you have success.**
>
> *Dr. Wayne Dyer*

You can even create a thought exchanging forum between yourself and your friends, *"Successors Thinking Club"* where like-minded business friends can think through such plans. Do not forget that succession plans should begin the day your child is born. Your club can meet every third monday of the month at 6 p.m., say, and you cannot only discuss amongst yourselves but also invite experts for a brainstorming session.

The club can be formed by just two people or more, but the membership should not exceed 16 or there will be less meaningful discussions and more noise.

Your wife is your best asset

Should your wife accompany you to the club meetings? It would all depend upon the mental framework of your wife. Do all you can to make your wife an integral part of any succession plan in your family business.

One of the most misunderstood and unappreciated assets in any family business is the wife of the owner-manager. The entrepreneur needs guts and talent to survive... and thrive. But he also needs a sympathetic and understanding wife. The wife of the business owner is his greatest asset potentially. He should share his dreams as well as his pains with her.

Katy Danco, who runs The Centre for Family Business along with her husband, Leon Danco says:

> *A successful family business is a dream in process, which can continue, generation after generation. Commitment, compassion, and contribution are the main ingredients of this stew of family relationships. A successful family business can reach its full potential only if the women in that family are willing to participate in the dream. Our husbands are doers, not discussers. This is why we have to become self-educated, active, not passive, listeners. Our role is to help our husbands to slow down and to enjoy what they have*

— especially their families. But first we have to encourage them to share their concerns. We must help them become "workalovics," not workaholics.

No matter how we get involved in our family business — through marriage, through birth, through inheritance, or through our own efforts, it quickly becomes an intimate part of our lives. To be happy and fulfilled, we are going to have to learn all the quirks of a family business, all of its demands, and then figure out how to live with them.

The family business adds a whole basket full of new problems to the burden each one of us already carries into our future. Often, we find ourselves cast into the role of making sure that everybody "runs together" at their own paces.

15

Delegate and... relax!

As the head of a family business, you can turn your successors into heroes or zeroes by the way you react to a situation. Sometimes, patience is the answer. Sometimes, an "acceptable level of dust" will do wonders. Here's how Dr. Danco puts it.

> *My mother, in my opinion, was the world's most dedicated housekeeper. People would be followed with the vacuum, ashtrays whisked away in mid-cigar, my Dad's socks were pressed, and the houseplants polished. That was the world in which I grew up.*
>
> *Then I got married. I remember one day being bothered by some dust on the piano. It didn't seem right. It drove me crazy. My wife had run an entire hospital floor. She was one of the few people I knew who came close to working harder than I did. But the dust on the piano was unacceptable to me. So I wrote "I love you" on it with my finger.*
>
> *Well, the house, as always, she kept clean, but she saw to it that my message and the little circle of dust she kept around it stayed on the piano for a couple of months. It took me that long to catch on! I eventually realised that no house is ever completely dust-free. It*

can always be improved, but at some point happiness requires some mutually acceptable level of "dust".

What usually prevents most business owners from delegating, leaving their hands off things, relaxing and finally retiring, is the inability to accept some dust. They can always see something wrong and they fix it. Other people seem always to leave more dust than they ever did. But what they fail to realise is that others don't do a worse job. They just tend to dust in different places, for different, reasons, under different priorities, at different times.

Now, most of us want our children to be like us and most of the time, it is the other way round. Think! Look around and you will come across funny situations. Your son doesn't resemble you 100 percent, does he? He did not grow up in your kind of environment. Then, how can he be like you? He has to be different.

Also, never forget that grooming your successor takes nine percent of your time thinking... imaginatively and creatively. Chance favours the prepared mind. Therefore, start preparing yourself from today irrespective of whether you are 36, 46 or 56. Good luck!

16
Small is beautiful

Now this is not meant to discourage you, but sometimes it does happen that your wife, sons, daughters — are either not competent enough or are not motivated enough to join the family business. Your situation could be something like this:

You sent your son to college in the nearest big city. You cut corners, saved hard and bought him a bicycle to go to college. Your son bought a mobike for his son in school. When it came to college, he sent his son to America to do an MBA.

Your grandson is back in India, as the vice-president of a multinational company. He earns his salary in dollars and drives a Puegeot. His wife wears short western dresses and goes to the nearest gym for aerobic classes. Your grandson talks of "liberalisation", "globalisation", "cyberspace" and the "the information highway". Half the time you don't understand what he is talking about because he uses so many abbreviations.

It is clear that your grandson has no interest in the family business which you and your son have been nurturing since many years. But don't despair. Times change and people move on.

Remember, fifty years ago you had refused to sit in your father's parchun ki dukan *(grocery store). Remember how you had insisted on studying for the matriculation and starting your own business. You must have hurt your father at that time. He couldn't understand why you wanted to do what you did. He worried about what you were getting yourself into. But he lived with it, didn't he? Later, he was even proud of your modest success in the new business. Try to remember how you basked in his unspoken pride.*

Next time you look at your grandson, try to look beyond the successful westernised exterior. He is no slick NRI. He is your own flesh and blood. So, accept him as he is — by lowering your standards.

THE JOY OF ROLE EXCELLENCE...

What you are hardly matters in role excellence. What matters is what you do with your role. Excellence need not be confined to what are considered "intelligent" or white collared roles. It is possible to have role excellence in every job, however humble. An excellent plumber is infinitely more admirable than an incompetent philosopher. The society, which scorns excellence in plumbing because it is a humble activity and tolerates shoddiness in philosophy because it is an exalted activity* will *have neither good plumbing nor good philosophy. Neither its pipes nor its theories will hold water.

It is not necessary that you have to become as big as Ford or Yamaha to enjoy the fruits of your business. You can still enjoy by remembering that *"Small is Beautiful,"* and maybe extend it to *"Small is Wonderful."* Please do not forget that you can earn more money and more respect with a 10-man set-up than by having a 100-man organisation.

A few years ago, Reliance Industries came up with an interesting advertisement, which gave a powerful message about the joy of role excellence (see box — The Joy of Role Excellence...).

Remember, it is more satisfying to see your loved ones achieve role excellence in whatever they do, instead of stepping in your shoes and being miserable all their lives.

The family you
come from isn't as
important as the family
you are going to have.

Ring Lardner

FOUR

Your relationship with your in-laws

After having met so many people from all walks of life, I have arrived at a simple, yet surprising fact — people find it most difficult to get along with their in-laws!

Why does this happen? Perhaps the root cause of our problems with our in-laws lies within us. We do not think twice when it comes to blaming them for our woes in life. They become our favourite punching bags. We fail to realise that, like every other relationship in life, our relationship with our in-laws needs delicate handling and constant care.

Most of us feel that our in-laws can never understand and accept us as well as our kith and kin. Often this very wrong notion about our in-laws prevents us from working wholeheartedly on our relationship with them. We fail to realise that we need to focus on cultivating a one-on-one relationship with our in-laws, instead of blaming them for most of our problems.

We can take small steps, in our own simple ways, to love and respect our in-laws, instead of losing our head and getting into skirmishes with them over little things.

The most important lesson I have learnt in my lifetime is — if you can't get along with your in-laws, you end up making not only them, but others in your family unhappy too!

So, do all you can to nurture your relationship with your in-laws. Remember, love is the only force capable of transforming a difficult in-law into an ally. Start trying to foster a bond of warmth, patience and empathy with your in-laws from today. Good Luck!

17

Change your wavelength

One day when Akbar and Birbal were out hunting, the emperor pointed to a crooked tree and asked, "Why is that tree crooked?"

Birbal answered, "That tree is crooked because it is the son-in-law of all the trees in the forest."

"Why do you say that?" asked Akbar.

Birbal quoted a proverb, "A dog's tail and a son-in-law are always crooked."

Akbar retorted, "Is my son-in-law also crooked?"

"Of course, Your Majesty!" said Birbal.

"Then have him crucified," ordered Akbar.

A few days later, Birbal had three crosses made — one of gold, one of silver and one of copper.

Akbar asked, "What are these for?"

Birbal answered, "Your Majesty, one of them is for you, one for me, and one for Your Majesty's son-in-law."

"But why are we to be crucified?" asked Akbar.

"Because," said Birbal, "we are all the sons-in-law of someone."

Akbar laughed and said, "Well then, let my son-in-law go."

This dialogue between Akbar and Birbal teaches us a simple truth — you cannot reform the world. You can't change your boss, your colleagues, your wife, your husband, your sons and daughters, or your friends. So what makes you think you can change your in-laws?

And since you can't change them, you have to learn to live with them if yours is a joint family set-up. And even if you don't live under the same roof, some *milna-julna* (interaction) is inevitable. Since you can't change your in-laws, the best thing you can do is change your attitude towards them. It is like listening to the radio and getting a crackly sound. If you change the knob around a little bit, you can get the station of your choice giving perfect sound quality. Sometimes it is more profitable to change your "wavelength" to suit the other person. Such change is not compromise; it is wisdom. And the wise are ready to do anything for peace.

By a sweet tongue and kindness, you can drag an elephant with a hair.

There are all kinds of people in this world — some kind, others not so kind. Be kind to unkind people — they need it the most. Similarly, there are all kinds of in-laws. If you are unfortunate enough to be saddled with an unkind in-law, follow your *dharma* to the best of your ability and leave the rest to God. The hardest of hearts can melt with unwavering good faith. Always remember, kindness is never wasted. If it has no effect on the recipient, at least it benefits the bestower. No matter what the situation, make it your resolution to lie down every night and be able to say: "I tried my best."

18

Don’t blow your top

Do you flare up at the slightest bit of friction? If you do, you had better stop this matchstick behaviour and learn to *keep your head* instead of losing it at the slightest provocation.

Family life has its share of ups and downs, domestic dramas, personality clashes, the lot. Don’t you remember having arguments with your own parents, brothers and sisters before you got married? So what is so terrible or even earth-shattering about disagreeing with your in-laws? Do you have to flare up and cause a full-scale fire just because they are your in-laws? Okay, you are having some trouble with your in-laws, but that is no reason for you to lose your head. Instead of being like a matchstick, learn a lesson from the *diya* (clay lamp). It burns quietly, slowly and steadily till the last drop of oil. Only then does it begin to splutter and waver. Learn not to react violently on impulse; instead learn to be patient like the *diya.*

Taking offense is a choice. We may be hurt, but there is a big difference between being hurt and taking offense.

Analyse your behaviour

In most quarrels there is fault on both sides. You can’t

clap with only one hand. Remember this when you are cursing fate for giving you such "bad" in-laws. Examine your own behaviour. If 60% of the fault lies with them, think about how you can further minimise the 40% of your share. Or is it that 60% of the blame lies with you? Think rationally. Do a quick self-analysis periodically. Are you to blame for the last shouting match you had with your in-laws? What was your contribution to the bad blood between you and them? It always pays do a sort of self-audit. Ask yourself: *"Where have I gone wrong? Could I have done anything to avoid this quarrel?"*

Life is not black and white; there are many shades of grey in between. Too often we spend too much time and energy in blaming each other. *Saas* and *bahu* get into needless little skirmishes over the smallest of issues and lock horns for the most trivial of reasons. Must these battles occur? Shouldn't we stop saying, *"I didn't do anything; it is all her fault."*

We get so caught up in these daily battles, we don't stop to think about the fixture of the family as a whole. So, the next time you find yourself in the middle of an argument or a disagreement with your in-laws, regardless of who is wrong, apologise and say, *"I am sorry I upset you."* These are healing, magical words.

Time cures all sorrows and quarrels because we all change and after some time what seems like a *mahabharat* or a *ghamasan yudh* (fierce battle) will seem like no more than a minor disagreement. It all depends on the right perspective.

19

Why sacrifice your king for a pawn

You are fed up with the daily battles over small things with your in-laws. But life has to go on. So what do you do? Become a bad-tempered person on the verge of a nervous breakdown? No you don't. Not if you are like the clever crow who wanted to drink from the bottom of a deep pot. He used pebbles to raise the level of water till he could reach the surface of water and drink his fill. Use your imagination to look around for solutions, just like the clever crow did. No situation, no matter how bad, is ever so hopeless that it has no scope for improvement.

Let me share with you a few of my *bramhastras* I use to tide over difficult situations in life.

Adopt "kee farak painda"

Some things are just not worth getting worked up over. For the small things that don't really matter, make it a policy to say *kee farak painda* (how does it matter?). Learn to shrug away these minor roadblocks to happiness.

> **Most of the shadows of this life are caused by standing in our own sunshine.**
>
> *Ralph Waldo Emerson*

Save the really important things

— such as matters of life and death, questions that compromise your honesty and integrity — for the *bahut farak painda* (it matters a lot!) category. In such cases stick to your guns and let nothing undermine your resolve.

In day-to-day dealing with in-laws you will find that 99% of all potentially explosive situations are of the KFP kind. Only 1% are BFP. Marriage has often been compared to a game of chess. And as any good chess player will tell you, you have to sacrifice the pawns to save the king, queen and bishops. You may have disagreements with your in-laws over many things. Sometimes they will do things your way; at other times you will have to do things their way.

There's no sense in losing your peace of mind over minor battles. Give in on where to put the TV, which colour to choose for the walls, what to cook for dinner. But in more important matters — such as which school to send your children to, or how to discipline them if they are getting spoilt, take a firm stand.

Make "this too shall pass" your motto

Make "this too shall pass" your motto when the going gets tough. Shed a few tears in solitude, if that makes you feel better, but don't let it get you down. Your "bad patch" with your in-laws could be due to various reasons — financial worries, ill-health, lack of personal space or privacy. Often, many of these reasons are beyond your control. When you have not contributed to these problems in any way, and cannot do anything to remove them, console yourself with the thought — this too shall pass.

However, respecting your in-laws is all very well. But when you find that your politeness is being mistaken for weakness, or that you are being ill-treated or taken for granted, call a halt. A daughter-in-law who puts up with her mother-in-law's biting, sharp comments every day is no better than a doormat. A father-in-law who constantly criticises his son-in-law can be the curse of a man's life. Be as fair and patient as you can be. But if there is no let up from the other side, find a way of putting an end to unnecessary unpleasantness.

Focus on the pluses

Remember, there is much more to marriage than the fun and excitement of shopping, buying clothes and jewellery, the *baraat* and *band baaja* followed by the honeymoon in Kulu Manali or Goa. The serious business of *being married* (instead of just *getting married)* starts when you return from the honeymoon and start living with a brand-new husband or wife and a brand-new readymade, fully grown-up family.

Marriage is no bed of roses. It requires plenty of hard work, dollops of tact, good humour, patience and maturity to make a marriage work.It is not important that you "love" your in-laws; what is important is that you work long and hard to have a good working relationship with them.

A good memory is one that can remember a day's blessings and forget the day's troubles.

Start your married life with the resolution that you will try to look for good points in your in-laws. There is no doubt that living with your in-laws is a tough balancing act. But, like the *madariwala,* with practice and patience, you too can master it.

Don't turn your in-laws into scapegoats

You have to learn to adapt to your in-laws blindspots. The most cardinal rule of a happy marriage is — whenever you fight with your better-half don't blame your in-laws for raising your spouse badly! Because if you do, it becomes a vicious circle. Both of you end up trading insults about your respective in-laws and the situation just goes from bad to worse.

Blaming or insulting each other's parents and family never brought any happiness to a marriage. So, keep the mention of in-laws strictly out of bounds in any husband-wife *tu-tu-main-main* (bickering).

The mind can make a heaven of hell, and a hell of heaven.

John Milton

Let's talk about another situation. You don't like your wife's father — for whatever reason. But you have to learn to keep your thoughts to yourself and show respect — for your wife's sake and for the children.

Children are like little pitchers with big ears. They hear most things you say and repeat them to others. To maintain peace in the family, be very careful of what you say in front of your children.

Also, look at it from the other side. Would *you* like it if, when your daughter gets married, her husband thinks that *you* are old and stupid?

20

Be a wise daughter-in-law

Don't turn your children into pawns

Some daughters-in-law make the mistake of turning their children into pawns in their on-going battles with the in-laws. Don't do that. It is counter-productive and harmful for the children. Also, it is very foolish on your part. Sometimes children can be an ideal bridge between you and your in-laws because you love your children and so do they. During a "cold war" children can help to keep channels of communication open.

Remember, your in-laws are not your enemies. They are not out to snatch your children away. A grandparent, no matter how loving, occupies a different though no less important compartment. If your children love their grandparents, it does not mean they love *you* any less.

> **If we do what is necessary, all the odds are in our favour.**
>
> *Henry Kissinger*

Encourage your children to be close to their grandparents. There is a lot they can learn from the grandparents — values such as caring, sharing and giving — which they will never find in textbooks or schools and colleges. Grandparents are, in some ways, better teachers than parents, for they have at their command a wealth of wisdom distilled from experience.

In our country there is an old saying: *"Asal se pyara sood"* (interest is dearer than the principal amount). In their old age, grandparents have all the time in the world to devote to their grandchildren. Often, they care more deeply for their grandchildren than they did for their own children. Don't deprive your in-laws of the sheer pleasure of spending time with their *nati-poti* (grandchildren).

Grandparents are the world's best baby-sitters. Nobody can match their genuine affection and care. For jet-setting parents leading hectic lives, the best thing they can offer their children is constant contact with a loving grandparent.

So, stop glaring at your in-laws when they hug their grandchildren or buy special gifts for them. They are not out to bribe your children and steal their affection. They can be a big support when it comes to raising your children.

Your in-laws' secrets are yours too!

Like Narad Muni, the character in mythology, who created a lot of misunderstanding as he could not keep any secrets, the telephone can sometimes play the role of Narad Muni in causing mischief in a family. Sometimes, daughters-in-law, especially the young and inexperienced ones, pick up the telephone and chatter endlessly with their mothers, telling them everything that is going on in their in-laws' house. What's cooked for dinner, the latest proposal for her youngest sister-in-law, the fight between her eldest brother-in-law and his wife, what the *dhobi* said to her mother-in-law, what the boss said to her husband — everything is poured down the line into mummy's eager, listening ears.

This is the worst mistake any daughter-in-law can make. Every home has its share of problems. There is no point in discussing your family problems with outsiders. It is like washing dirty linen in public. Keep your problems within the *char diwari* (four walls) of your home. With tons of tact and patience, these small obstacles to happiness can be removed.

> **We cannot always control our thoughts, but we can control our words, and repetition impresses the subconscious, and we are then masters of the situation.**
>
> *Horence Scoril Shinn*

Learn to be discreet. Don't gossip, certainly not with your mother. Once you are married into a family, their secrets are your secrets. You have to respect their privacy. Don't turn a kitty party into a *"Let's bitch about our mothers-in-laws,"* session.

Remember, *Nanak dukhiya sab sansar* (Oh, Nanak, everyone in this world has problems!). There is very little to be gained by cribbing about your family problems, domestic dramas and marital anxieties with anyone unless he or she can help or guide you in a constructive way.

Let your husband play Sravan Kumar

Over the centuries, every man nurtures a desire to be like Sravan Kumar to his parents. If your husband wants to do it too, let him do it to his heart's content. A happy son is a good husband and a good father. Problems arise when he feels thwarted from being a good son, or when he feels that you are not letting him be Sravan Kumar.

Have patience. Remember what Aristotle said: *"Patience is bitter, but its fruit is sweet."* Don't make snide remarks or unkind references about your husband carrying the "load" of your in-laws on his shoulders. With each little dig you will be digging your own marital grave.

> **Do a little more each day than you think you possibly can.**
> *Lowell Thomas*

One good side effect of all this will be that when your sons and daughters see their father looking after his parents, they too will do the same when your time comes. In a family where grandparents and older relatives are respected, children pick up the right values. In homes where the elderly are neglected, children grow up to be adults with a coarse moral fibre.

Don't show off

As a daughter-in-law you should not forget the wise saying, *Jitni chadar ho, utne paon pasaro* (figuratively speaking, it means spend within your means). If your in-laws can't afford to buy expensive gifts and gadgets, don't ask your father to pamper you. Above all, don't flaunt your father's wealth in front of your in-laws. It is sign of bad manners and is called "showing-off". It will prick your in-laws where it hurts most — their self-respect.

Don't forget, life is a series of trade-offs. As a *bahu* (daughter-in-law) you have many duties to perform and even if they are not an essential part of the relationship, they are priceless as far as making your in-laws happy is concerned.

21

Invest time in your in-laws... now

All relationships — with friends, neighbours, colleagues, business associates — need a lot of careful nurturing. So why not the relationship with in-laws? In-laws are in the unfortunate position of being not quite the same as family and are seldom considered friends. We neither feel the spontaneous love for them that we do for our blood relations or immediate family, nor are we willing to give them the time and importance that we give to our friends.

Here lies our first and most serious mistake. Relations with in-laws have to be watered with plenty of care, patience and understanding. Invest time in your in-laws. It will bear rich dividends. In the bargain, it will make your stock with them soar. It is a guaranteed, time-tested win-win deal.

> **One-on-ones are where most of the real work of the family is done. This is where there is the deepest nurturing of heart and soul.**

Each of us is sure to be someone's son-in-law or daughter-in-law or father-in-law or mother-in-law or sister-in-law or brother-in-law. And since most people, statistically speaking, are neither wicked nor mean, there is no rule that says all in-laws are necessarily bad.

Why, then, is there such a fear of in-laws? Why are

in-laws the butt of so many nasty jokes? Why are they always cast as the villains in every domestic melodrama in homes across the length and breadth of the country? A lot, perhaps, has to do with Bollywood masala films, which routinely show the mother-in-law pulling the *bahu* by the *choti* and making her work like a slave. The *bahu* too is typecast in one of these two roles: the *sati-savitri bhartiya nari* who takes everything without a murmur of protest; or the bold and brazen modem miss who boots out the in-laws and has the husband wrapped around her little finger.

Both versions are far from the truth. In-laws are human beings like everyone else. It is a pity that in India a young girl's mind gets poisoned against her in-laws even before the wedding. Go to any *Ladies' Sangeet* on the night before a wedding and you will hear women, young and old, singing naughty songs about the girl's would-be in-laws. Wedding songs, folk songs, Hindi film songs — they all condition young girls to believe that the in-laws are to be feared, even hated.

He who speaks evil of another, cannot find the way of peace.

There are numerous jokes on the subject of the in-laws (especially mothers-in-law). For example, you may have seen a certain kind of cactus with long, sharp leaves. The leaves are green with yellow borders; the edges are sharp and thorny. The plant is called a mother- in-law's tongue!

In-laws are undoubtedly the cornerstone of all successful marriages. I am not saying you must *love* your in-laws; I am simply saying that you must learn to co--exist happily with a minimum of tension. A good working-relationship with the in-laws is important if you want to keep your wife or husband or daughter or son happy. Don't forget, it is the little things that go a long way in paving the way for the big and important things.

Little things that matter

Making a hot cup of tea for your father-in-law first thing in the morning — with no sugar and lots of milk, just the way he likes it — is a very little thing. But if you do it with *lagan* (devotion) and give it to him with a smile, you may start his day on a bright note. And that is a very big thing.

> **Great things are not done by an impulse but by a series of small things brought together.**
>
> *Vincent Van Gogh*

- *If your mother-in-law sends you a Kancheepuram saree by speed post for your wedding anniversary, a prompt thank you will please her as much as it pleased you to receive the beautiful silk saree. So, pick up the phone and call her, now.*
- *If you, as a son-in-law, have been extra nice to your father-in-law, your wife will look at you with new eyes.*
- *If you, as a* bahu, *have made that little bit of extra effort in your relationship with your mother-in-law, your husband will respect you that little bit more.*

Any relationship with your in-laws is a two-way street. If you take without giving, you are going to reach a dead-end. On the other hand, if you maintain constant give-and-take — not necessarily of expensive gifts; it can be a phone call, a bunch of flowers, cards on birthdays and anniversaries or letters — you keep the channels of communication open.

Do whatever you can to make sure that your in-laws do not feel unappreciated or taken-for-granted. Thoughtful little gestures will go a long way in nurturing a healthy relationship with your in-laws. Like rare and exotic plants, in-laws too need delicate handling and constant care.

Too much honesty can create problems

You could do well to remember that with in-laws, as in all human relationships, too much honesty can, and often does, create problems. These delicately balanced relationships require that we blunt the sharp cutting edge of truth — with diplomacy and tact. Let me give you a few examples of how you can deal with dicey situations.

> **Your loved ones act like a mirror: they force you to look at everything about yourself that is not loving, and then they stretch you into learning to love more.**
>
> *Barbara De Angelis*

Suppose your mother-in-law walks in wearing a new saree. You think it is terrible but she thinks it is lovely. Moreover, she is excited at buying it at a sale and is thrilled with her purchase. So, what do you do? Do you tell her it is a horrible colour and doesn't suit her, or seeing that she is so happy wear-

ing it, you say something tactful like: "It is certainly a striking colour." I would not dampen her spirits if I were you.

Take another situation. Your sister-in-law has cooked Chinese food for dinner according to a new recipe she has learnt from Khana Khazana for which she had to stand in the kitchen for hours.

You hate Chinese food but the least you can do is taste a little and appreciate it. For her sake.

> **A sound relationship is not based on complete frankness; it is based on tact.**
> *M. Ernst*

When honesty is tempered with good manners and compassion, it shows that you care. And if you have to live peacefully under one roof, it is the most important thing you can show towards your new family.

Don't worry, be happy

In the final analysis, in any relationship with the in-laws, *deciding* to be happy is as important as *being* happy. If you allow the constant *kich-kich* (squabbling) to get you, you are bound to be stressful and unhappy.

> **There is no gathering the rose without being pricked by the thorns.**

On the other hand, if you tell yourself happiness is a state of mind and has nothing to do with the actual, physical environment you live in, the smiles and laughter will come back into your life.

Find something to divert your mind. Take up a new hobby or join a course. Remember, happiness is the result of being too busy to be miserable. So, next time you squabble with your mother-in-law over the maid or the *dhobi*; or you find yourself at loggerheads with your sister-in-law over whose turn it is to make the *rotis*; or you get angry when you see your father-in-law picking his nose in front of your smart friends... think before you flare up. In all likehood thinking cool-headedly will make you realise that such petty issues are not worth staking your happiness for.

22

When you become a parent-in-law

Nothing can be more disastrous for a family than a marriage based on greed or false expectations. Young men have been known to exercise very bad judgement in picking a mate. So have daughters often got entangled with the wrong sort of men who expect the in-laws to support their luxurious lifestyle.

Such things have happened before. They will happen again. Still, in most cases, we have to work hard to keep the channels of communication open. There's no point in saying, *"I can't stand him (or her), so what's the use of talking?"* Once your children have made their choice of a spouse, you will only be making a foolish mistake if you force them to choose between you and the young man or woman they have married.

The rebellious daughter-in-law

Take the case of the rebellious daughter-in-law, who refuses to adjust, adapt or even listen to reason. Her problems may be real or imaginary. It will help if her in-laws start thinking of their son's wife as "one of us," not as "her" or "that woman he married." She is the mother of their grandchildren and cannot remain an outsider, even though she comes to their family as a stranger.

Rebellion is often a cry for attention. Perhaps if somebody sat down with her and tried to find out what is pricking her like a thorn all the time, she could be helped to get over whatever is causing her to behave difficult.

Every act of rebelling expresses a nostalgia for innocence and an appeal to the essence of being.

Daughters-in-law deserve much more attention than they normally get. It is only when they get attention that they develop a sense of belonging. It is one thing to say that she is part of the family. Most people say it, as this is the expected, obvious thing to say. But to accept her as a part of the family takes a lot of patience. Once she feels fully accepted, her rebellion will go away — just like pimples from a teenager's face.

Must you compare?

If your son-in-law does not live up to your expectations don't make him feel small and inadequate by comparing him with other better-placed members of the family. If you are in the habit of doing so, you are surely chopping away at the very roots of your daughter's marriage and shaking its foundation.

Mutual respect is the foundation for any secure marriage. If your daughter hears you comparing her husband with others and his coming out in a poor light, she too will lose respect for her husband. That is when quarrels and bickering begin to corrode away at a marriage.

Stay out of your daughter's married life. If you have any reservations about your son-in-law — keep them to yourself. *Uski saree meri se safed kaise?* (how is her saree whiter than mine?) is all very well when the comparison is about washing powder, but when you start saying *Uski amdani teri amdani se zyada kaise?* (how is his salary more than yours?), you are making a very serious blunder.

Nagging never helps

In many homes the son and daughter-in-law work while the children are looked after by the grandparents. One large happy family, you might say. But not quite. A closer look often shows the cracks beneath the surface.

> **To find fault is easy; to do better may be difficult.**
> *Plutarch*

The daughter-in-law gets up at the crack of dawn. She makes a pile of *paranthas* for the family's breakfast, cooks lunch for the in-laws, packs tiffin boxes, and then catches a bus to rush to office. In the evening, after putting in eight hours of work she comes back. But she can't afford to put up her feet and relax; she makes tea, cooks dinner, helps the children with homework. At the end of a 24-hour day into which she packs 36 hours of hectic work, she is frazzled and bone-tired. Then her mother-in-law starts — the *chapatis* for lunch were half-burnt, the house hasn't been dusted, a button is missing on her husband's shirt, the *dal* has too much salt... nag, nag, nag. Sounds dramatic? Well, it happens and in such an unpleasant environment, children suffer the most.

Children, no matter how small, have giant computers fitted inside their heads. If they watch their mother looking tired and unhappy all the time, being nagged and picked on, it is going to tell on them. So, if for no other reason, for the sake of your grandchildren, stop nagging your daughter-in-law. Take a little of the burden off her shoulders. It will make for a happier home.

Saas bhi kabhi bahu thi

Life would be so much simpler if mothers-in-law stopped resenting their daughters-in-law for taking their sons away. The truth is that no one and nothing can take your son away from you. A wife occupies a different "compartment" and can never take your place in your son's affections.

> **Real magic in relationships means an absence of judgement of others.**
>
> *Dr. Wayne Dyer*

Remember that old Hindi film — *Saas bhi kabhi bahu thi* (the mother-in-law was once a daughter-in-law). Remember your own time when you were young and just starting out in your married life. Remember the countless mistakes you made when you first left the sheltered home of your parents and stepped into your husband's huge joint family. The countless adjustments, big and small, the many heartaches, the stream of relatives — how you coped with everything till today you are in the position of having a grown up son and a brand-new *bahu.*

So, wisen up. And loosen up. Stop glaring at your poor daughter-in-law every time she dresses up and greets your son wearing a new dress or a bright smile. She is not trying to snatch your *laadla* (apple of your eye) away. She is not your enemy. She can, if you let her, become your closest ally.

Don't be too harsh on her. Give her time. Don't jump down her throat at the smallest pretext. She will turn out OK — just as you did.

Children are not so
different from kites...
children were created to
fly. But they need wind —
the undergirding and strength
that comes from unconditional
love, encouragement,
and prayer.

Gigi Graham Tchividjian

FIVE

Nuture your grandchildren with love

There are many ways in which you can measure your success as a grandparent. One of my personal favorites is when I chance upon my grand-children describing me — their grandpa —while talking to their friends.

I am elated when they tell their buddies that I am their friend — someone they can relate to. I feel grateful to them for having accepted me as an equal in their world of bubbly innocence. Years seem to slip away from me in a moment and I look forward to enjoying every minute with them. When I play with my grandchildren Gayatri, Gaurav and Ananya, it seems like paradise on earth.

As a contended grandparent, let me share a simple pearl of wisdom with you — a grandchild is a "bonus" which God has given to us. The best way we can take care of this special gift from the Almighty is to nurture him or her with love.

I rejoice in the simple pleasures of life with my grandchildren by playing with them, enjoying them and spoiling them — a wee bit. The mere fact that I have lived long enough to be blessed with grandchildren, who make me feel young and full of enthusiasm, has led to happiness in my life. It has also helped me spread happiness to others.

As a grandparent, you must realise that your grandchildren look up to you as their role model. Your attitudes will strongly influence their attitudes for better or worse. The best way you can teach your grandchildren the right values in life is by setting good examples for them.

Preaching and comparing your grandchildren with yourself when your were their age will not make the bond between you and your grandchildren stronger. It is unrealistic to compare them with what you were 60 years ago! Besides, your grandchildren are far smarter than you ever were. So, learn to accept your grandchildren as they are.

23

Welcome your "winter of content"

You have retired from your job. Or you have handed over the reins of the family business to your sons. Grey hair and maturity have lent you an air of serenity and as John Keats said, you are approaching the period of "mellow fruitfulness".

You are readying yourself for the autumn of your life when your first grandchild arrives. By the time he or she grows up and other grandchildren begin to arrive, you are well into the winter of your "content". What better time than this to recapture your childhood through your grandchildren? They are, after all, your passports to eternal youth.

Raising children can be a harrowing job — fraught with worries, inexperience and the nagging thought: "Am I doing it right?" But by the time your grandchildren come along you have become adept at dealing with people and situations. You have learnt most of life's lessons at the School of Hard Knocks.

> **Children are the living messages we send to a time we will not see.**
>
> *John W. Whitehead*

As grandparents, you have at your command a wealth of wisdom distilled over the ages from *kisse kahaniyan,* stories from the *Ramayana* and *Mahabharata,* tales about

Akbar and Birbal, and above all, drawn from your own experience of life. There is a very thought provoking saying, *"For the ignorant old age is winter; for the wise it is harvest time."* So, take part in the simple unadulterated pleasures, which your grandchildren provide. It is through all this that you can pass on something beyond worldly riches and wealth to your grandchildren — the right set of values.

You may be a crorepati with a string of houses and farms and a stable-full of expensive cars. Your wife and daughters-in-law may wear designer clothes and Cartier jewellery, but if your sons quarrel among themselves and your grandchildren are spoilt brats, are you really successful? Sure you are a rich man who will be leaving behind a vast inheritance one day. But apart from all your wealth and real estate, what have you done to leave behind the invaluable legacy of a well-brought-up family?

You will be remembered not for the money in your Swiss accounts, your offices and factories, not even the multi-million rupee deals you made.... but for the values you left behind and the sort of people your children and grandchildren grow up to be.

Inculcate the right values

Just like a potter with wet clay, you too can mould your grandchildren. Use your invaluable experience to instill the right values in your grandchildren. Teach them old-fashioned but never-out-of-use values such as selflessness, honesty, sincerity, sharing, empathy... Teach them all those things that their parents are too busy to worry about and also things that never feature in any school curriculum. Teach them to ask, from time to time, life's most persistent question: *"What are we doing for others?"*

The more a child feels valued, the better his values will be.

Tell them about the little things that matter, the little things that people caught up in the rat race have forgotten. Tell your grandchildren things they will cherish later in life. Tell them to be prepared to lose once in a while. Tell them success is never final and failure never fatal. Above all, tell them, the time of failure is the best time for sowing the seeds of success. Tell them all this and more, for they will eagerly listen to you. Their minds are young and supple. Each word of yours will leave a lasting impression.

24

Be there when your grandchildren need you

Your presence is vital

In families where parents lead hectic lives, grandparents can step into the breach and give their grandchildren the attention they require. When busy parents try to placate a problem child with gifts and toys, grandparents can play a far more useful role by reaching to the root of the problem. If at a young age a child has been identified as a "problem child" or a "spoilt brat," grandparents can find out what makes the child behave in that way. Often tears and temper tantrums are a child's distress signal; if heeded in time, many problems can be avoided later.

> **Too much love never spoils children. Children become spoiled when we substitute "presents" for "presence".**
>
> *Dr. Anthony P. Witham*

Say, your son and daughter-in-law are both busy, working people. They either forget your grandchild's PTA meeting or simply can't make it to the school sports day as it clashes with an important meeting.

But *you* can make it. You are there to cheer your grandchild when he or she comes in third in the 50-m dash. You clap the loudest even when your grandchild makes a 30-second appearance in the school play. You do this because it is your way of telling your grandchild that it is not the winning that counts; participation is just as important.

> **The best things you can give children, next to good habits, are good memories.**
> *Sydney J. Harris*

Your presence on such occasions is vital. Don't say *kee pharak painda* whether I go or not. Ask your grandchild. I am sure he or she will say: *Bahut pharak painda!* A smile, a word of appreciation, a pat of encouragement from you can make all the difference between winning and losing for your grandchild.

Let's take another example. Your grandson needs help with his homework. He has to write a 100-word essay on the Red Fort. Take time off from reading your company report or whatever you are doing, to help him write it. You may disagree with what I am saying. It may make more sense to you to pay someone Rs. 300 a month to tutor your grandchild in the evenings. But in the long run, it doesn't pay.

All your grandchild is asking for is some guidance; the rest he can manage on his own. Besides, and this is more important, he probably wants to spend some time with you which is why he approaches your desk, school bag in hand. Recognise the real *need* behind the request. Your grandchild wants to sit beside you and finish his essay. So, give him a few minutes of your valuable time. Later on when he looks back on his childhood, it is these precious moments that will stay in his memory.

25

You can be a great buddy

Grandchildren value the company of their grandparents just as much as grandparents enjoy their childish prattle. Grandparents would be doing their grandchildren and themselves a great disservice if they think of themselves as worthless old timers. Grandchildren are more friendly and comfortable in the company of their grandparents than parents. The reason is, perhaps, because grandparents have already used up all their anxieties in raising their own kids and are therefore, more stress-free and less prone to constantly breathing down the necks of the their grandchildren. Experience has taught them to be more relaxed and less tense about minor worries.

This feeling of space and freedom from constant checks and controls can create a feeling of companionship between grandparents and grandchildren. A grandchild can sometimes confide more easily in a grandparent than in his father or mother. This sense of easy companionship makes them enjoy doing things together such as going for a walk or playing a game of chess. Such occasions not only give mutual satisfaction but serve as useful "pressure valves". Grandchildren can let off steam about things that worry them. Grandparents often become good sounding boards for new ideas.

Grandchildren don't need expensive holidays abroad,

trips to Disneyland or high-tech entertainment parks. Summer vacations spent with grandparents who are lively and interested in them can be great fun. This can be a very refreshing holiday for both grandchildren and grandparents. Grandchildren can have unending fun exploring parks, museums, going on excursions, picnics, watching old films, going for walks with a grandparent who can point out interesting things and be their "window to the world". Grandparents, too feel lively and excited, seeing things afresh from a child's point of view. It can be the best prescription for all their old-age aches and pains.

> **A great man is he who has not lost the heart of a child.**
>
> *Mencius*

So, if you are a grandparent, plan special treats and outings with your grandchildren. Spend your days in simple pleasures... such as sitting on a park bench, feeding birds, playing with your grandchildren, enjoying their company. It will add pep and vigour to your life and give you a new reason to be active.

Relive your lost innocence through your grandchildren's happy gurgles. Sometimes, getting up in the morning and asking your grandchild, "*What shall we do today?*" can be better than any tonic or pick-me-up. You are only as young or as old as you feel. And in the company of children, you can feel really very young.

Mail A Special Thought

Children love to get things in the mail. From the time they are four-plus and able to read their name, nothing gives them greater pleasure than to see their name written on a stamped envelope, being delivered by the postman.

So, if your grandchildren live away from you, or even if they live in the same city, send them a card or letter, or even a surprise gift through the mail. It forms an instant bond. The child, too, feels happy and proud to receive something special through a letter, from a special buddy.

Thank God for grandchildren!

Thank God for your grandchildren. Don't try to change them or burden them with the weight of your own hopes and aspirations. Instead, get to know them, and adapt yourself.

In big cities with western-style nuclear families you can be your grandchildren's sole link to the great storehouse of Indian folklore. Traditionally passed on from one generation to the next by word of mouth, folk-tales combine earthy wisdom with fairy tales. Such stories teach children what is never taught in schools — values such as caring, sharing, loving and giving.

The story of Sravan Kumar, the playful god Krishna Kanhaiya, Sheikh Chilli, the wise fool, Akbar, Savitri and Satyavan, and countless others convey all the magic and excitement of India — a land steeped in folklore and tradition.

Remember, grandchildren are given to you — on loan

— for a very short period of time. They come to you like packets of seeds, with no guarantees. You do not know what they have the potential to become. It is not important for grandchildren to just grow up (for even a tree can grow), but to grow up well. You can do a lot to make sure that your grandchildren grow up to be fine human beings. Your job as a grandparent is to be like a good gardener — to meet your grandchildren's needs as best you can, give them proper nourishment, love, attention and care, and hope for the best.

26

Be in tune with today

Prickly teenagers... handle with care

So you don't approve of your teenaged granddaughter wearing sleeveless blouses and short skirts? Or your teenaged grandson driving fast cars and going on dates? You grumble to yourself or complain to your friends who have similar problems, "*Things were different in my time. I was already married and with kids when I was their age. These days children don't seem to know the meaning of responsibility.*"

If your grandchildren are really as bad as you perceive them to be, do some hard thinking. Where were you when they were growing up? If they have gone astray, it is perhaps because no one was there to teach them right from wrong.

Let's discuss another common problem. Your teenaged granddaughter is always talking on the phone. You are horrified at the expense; you are amazed that her parents (your son and daughter-in-law) aren't able to control her; moreover, you are at a loss to understand how she can talk for hours on end.

So what do you do? Do you shout at her and tell her that in your days girls were seen but never heard? Threaten to disconnect the phone? Make snide digs at your daughter-in-law for not being a proper influence on a growing girl?

Life is ambiguous; there are many right answers — all depending on what you are looking for. But if you think there is only one right answer, then you will stop looking as soon you find one.

No, if you are wise you do none of these things. Instead, you talk to her to find out what her interests are and encourage your granddaughter to develop hobbies. You try, gently and patiently, to encourage her to read books and magazines, get her talking about her school or college, her friends and her dreams for the future. If you show her ways to channelise her energies constructively, you may be able to wean her away from this wasteful pastime. You could also do some basic arithmetic and point out, tactfully, how much one phone call that lasts for hours can cost.

So, it all boils down to thinking positively. Things may not be as bad as they seem. Just because your grand-children wear peculiar clothes, listen to loud music, drive fast cars, it does not mean they are bad kids. Sure, like Maggi's Tomato Sauce, they are *different.* They are different from what young people used to look like and talk about fifty years ago. But then, remember, times change. It w as a wise man who once said, *"There is nothing permanent except change."*

27 Inspire your grandchildren

Be their role models

Children trust their eyes rather than their ears. The effect of preaching is slow and tedious on young minds. The conscience of children is formed by the influences around them; their ideas of good and bad are the result of the moral atmosphere they breathe. They will do what they see being done around them; they will believe in what they see their elders believing in. Children desperately need role models. They almost invariably look up to grandparents in search of idols.

The most precious gift grandparents can give their grandchildren is a good example. Grandparents can do more good by being good, than in any other way. If grandchildren look up to their grandparents, they have made a success of life's hardest job.

Grandparents can inspire their grandchildren to take the ups and downs of life in their stride by reading to them this thought-provoking poem called "*If...*" by Rudyard Kipling, which he wrote for his son.

If you can keep your head when all about you
Are losing theirs and blaming it on you,
If you can trust yourself when all men doubt you,

But make allowance for their doubting too;

If you can wait and not be tired by waiting,
Or being lied about, don't deal in lies,
Or being hated, don't give way to hating,
And yet don't look too good, nor talk too wise;

If you can dream — and not make dreams your master,
If you can think — and not make thoughts your aim,
If you can meet with Triumph and Disaster
And treat those two imposters just the same;
If you can bear to hear the truth you've spoken
Twisted by knaves to make a trap for fools,
Or watch the things you gave your life to, broken,
And stoop and build 'em up with worn-out tools;

If you can make one heap of all your winnings
And risk it on one turn of pitch-and-toss,
And lose, and start again at your beginnings
And never breathe a word about your loss;
If you can force your heart and nerve and sinew
To serve your turn long after they are gone,
And so hold on when there is nothing in you
Except the Will which says to them: 'Hold on!'

If you can talk with crowds and keep your virtue,
Or walk with kings — nor lose the common touch,
If neither foes nor living friends can hurt you,

If all men count with you, but none too much;
If you can fill the unforgiving minute
With sixty seconds' worth of distance run,
Yours is the Earth and everything that's in it,
And — which is more — you'll be a Man, my son!

28

Spare the pampering, love your grandchildren

You've had to fight tooth and nail for your success. You are where you are today because you battled against all odds and made it to the top. You look back and see one long, weary, back-bearing journey.

You look at your grandchildren and your heart swells with pride ... and also a sense of protection. You want to give them everything you never had. You want to make their life as easy as yours was difficult. But, wait, aren't you doing them a grave injustice? Aren't you pampering them, by giving them everything they could want.

> **A man who gives his children habits of industry provides for them better than by giving them a fortune.**
>
> *Richard Whately*

Giving your grandchild all the benefits of a good education and a fine upbringing is one thing, but for heaven's sake don't spoil them.

You turned out okay perhaps because you had to fight for what you wanted. Don't turn your grandchildren into weaklings by showering them with material things at too early an age. It is good to have the things that money can buy, but it is also good to check up once in a while and be sure that you have the things that money can't buy. Such as the genuine love of your near and dear ones.

When money is allowed to gain too much value, the first casualty is human relationships. Your grandchildren should love you for what you are; not for what you can give them.